"You're wicked with that knife."

"Knife skills are one of the best weapons in a chef's arsenal," Remy said.

Remy found the same comfort of working in the kitchen with Staci as he did in his own kitchen back home. But that didn't surprise him; he'd always known he was meant to be a chef. He just wasn't sure he was meant to follow his father's and uncles' culinary vision.

Staci distracted him and that intrigued him. He'd had affairs before—he was too passionate and his sexual drive was too high for him not to. But he'd never allowed himself an affair with another chef. It seemed to him that life was best served by keeping his personal and professional lives separate.

Now, he wasn't sure. He watched her dip her spoon into the sauce she was preparing and that tiny pink tongue of hers darted out to lick it. In his mind, he moved closer to her and tested the sauce, not from the spoon but from her lips.

"Want a taste?" she asked.

He snapped back to the present and nodded. He wanted way more than a taste, but that would be a good place to start. She held the spoon out to him but he too'...

Her li... his time t... was a rosy...

"Delic...

Dear Reader,

I'm obsessed. Not about anything naughty but about televised cooking competitions. I can watch them from the US, the UK and Australia and I do. I love the subtle nuances of each of the different shows. And I admire how, no matter what the country, the competitors are fierce. I can't get enough of watching the interaction of the contestants and wondering what if…?

What if one of the contestants was the son of a famous chef? What if he lied about who he was and what if, as happens in real life, he falls for a woman while living this lie? These are the seeds of the story that became *Sizzle*.

I hope you enjoy it!

Happy reading!

Katherine Garbera

SIZZLE

BY
KATHERINE GARBERA

First published in Great Britain 2013
by Mills & Boon, an imprint of Harlequin (UK) Limited,
Eton House, 18-24 Paradise Road, Richmond, Surrey TW9 1SR

© Katherine Garbera 2013

ISBN: 978 0 263 90508 3

30-0513

Harlequin (UK) policy is to use papers that are natural, renewable and recyclable products and made from wood grown in sustainable forests. The logging and manufacturing processes conform to the legal environmental regulations of the country of origin.

Printed and bound in Spain
by Blackprint CPI, Barcelona

Katherine Garbera is a *USA TODAY* bestselling author of more than forty books, who has always believed in happy endings. She lives in England with her husband, children and their pampered pet, Godiva. Visit Katherine on the web at www.katherinegarbera.com, or catch up with her on Facebook and Twitter.

It's funny how you can know someone her entire life and still be surprised by how much you still enjoy hanging out with her years later. This book is dedicated to my sister Donna. Love you, DD.

Special thanks to Kathryn Lye for insight in the early stages when I was going down a wrong path.

1

STACI ROWLAND RAN THE LAST block and a half to the Hamilton Ramsfeld kitchen and studios. She was late, more than late she was on the verge of blowing the chance of a lifetime—the chance to be on *Premier Chef*. And the chance to win half a million dollars and have her own television cooking show. The chance to get back into a Michelin starred kitchen and prove that all the raw young talent she'd had hadn't been wasted.

She was running late because she was a little short of money this week, which was her own fault because she'd blown every cent of her disposable income on a new set of knives for this competition. Gas prices were high and she hadn't been able to afford a tank of gas from San Diego to Santa Monica so instead she'd had to bus it.

Now sweat was dripping down her back, she was overheated and the knives she carried in her left hand were starting to feel as if they weighed a ton. She ran through the front doors of the building, air-conditioning immediately starting to cool her damp back. She glanced at the empty reception desk.

"Damn," she said, under her breath, rushing to the desk to find a clipboard with a list of names, including hers and instructions to take the elevator to the fourteenth floor. She pushed the elevator button and opened her purse to search for the letter she'd received from the Premier Chef producers, hoping it had an exact room number on it. The bell pinged and she stepped into the elevator car, catching the toe of her shoe on the lip of the gap, which sent her sprawling forward.

Staci cursed as she tumbled through the air expecting to hit the floor and instead hit a warm solid person. She heard his curse as a stream of cool liquid washed over both of them. She glanced up, an apology on her lips, and froze as she stared into a pair of Caribbean blue eyes. She tried to push herself free but her hand slipped on his arm and he gripped her waist to keep her upright.

"Oh fudge," she said. "I'm just not having a good day."

He was tall and, she could tell from the way he was holding her, well built with a muscled chest and strong shoulders. His jaw was square with an almost bullish set to it and when he looked down at her with those brilliant blue eyes of his, they were frosty. Not frosty enough to dry the sweat dripping down her back but she felt a definite chill. Great, she thought, it was as if the universe was conspiring to ruin her day.

"I'm sorry," she said.

"It's cool," he said, his southern drawl washed over her senses and she did a double take. He had casually ruffled dark black hair that curled over his forehead. His body was lean and muscular not typical of every chef she'd met. And she had no doubt that he was a chef. "Maybe next time you should look where you are going?"

"Thanks, I hadn't thought of that," she shot back. Not in a mood to be sweet and cheery since she was over-heated and as the liquid dried on her skin it felt sticky. "What were you drinking?"

"Sweet tea," he said.

Of course he was since his voice was all Southern plantations and magnolia trees she wasn't surprised. She brushed her hands over her clothes and shook her head. "Someone up there really hates me."

"Up there?" he asked, reaching around her to push the button for the fourteenth floor.

"The universe or heaven or whatever you like to call the fickle fates," she said, tucking a strand of her short hair behind her ear.

"Why are you blaming an unseen power when you are clearly running late?" he asked. "If you'd been here on time none of this would have happened."

"Touché," she said.

Silence grew between them and Staci tried to just let it be, but she hated quiet…always had.

"Are you here for the competition?" she asked. It was an educated guess, but one she suspected would be confirmed since he held a bag of chef knives in one hand.

"Yes," he said. "I hope you are better in the kitchen than you are in the elevator."

"Oh, you haven't seen me at my best in the elevator," she said with a wink. Then holding out her hand to him, she introduced herself. "I'm Staci Rowland."

"Remy…Stephens," he said. His handgrip was firm and his hand was warm in hers. His hands showed signs that he'd been a chef for a while with burn marks and nicks that had long since scarred over. If his hands were any indication the man could cook.

She stared at his face perhaps a little longer than she should, unable to look away from the beard stubble on his face, which gave him a rugged sexy appearance. When she glanced back at his eyes she saw that he'd lifted one eyebrow at her.

She dropped his hand and rubbed hers on her jean-clad leg. *What the hell was wrong with her today*?

"Oh, like that little mouse in *Ratatouille*," she said. Her niece loved that film and after they'd watched it together Louisa had insisted on having ratatouille for dinner.

"Ratatouille? The vegetable dish?"

"No," she said. "The Disney-Pixar movie. It's about a chef who is lost and finds his culinary way with the help of a little mouse named Remy."

"Um…no like my great-uncle," he said. "I don't watch animated movies."

She shrugged. "It's cute. You should give it a try."

She stepped further back to look at him. "Sorry again about bumping into you."

"No problem. I get messier in the kitchens," he said. "I'm just thinking about cooking today."

"Me, too," she said with a half-smile. "I'm the co-owner of Sweet Dreams, a cupcake bakery in San Diego."

"The cupcake girl," he said. "I read over the profiles of the other chefs this morning."

"Cupcake girl? My partner and I own a very profitable bakery…I'd rather not be referred to as the cupcake girl." She wished she'd thought to read the profiles as well, maybe then she'd know more about Remy. But as she'd been running late she hadn't had time.

Now he was the one to step back and gave her a low bow. "My most humble apologies, baker."

"Where do you work?" she asked.

"I'm sort of between gigs right now but I've worked in the best kitchens in New Orleans."

"I suspected as much," she said.

"How?"

"That slow Southern drawl of yours gave you away."

He gave her a slow steady smile that made her pulse kick up a notch. She couldn't put her finger on what it was but there was something familiar in his smile. Also something so damned sexy that she wondered if she should just get off at the next floor.

Some women were into men in uniforms, others into men with power and money but for her it had always been the earthy sensuality of a man who could cook.

"Do you like it?" he asked, his drawl even more pronounced than before.

She grinned back. "Maybe."

He arched one eyebrow at her. "Most people find my accent charming."

"Really?"

He gave her a measured look and then winked at her. "Cupcake girl, it's a big part of my personality," he said. "Some people underestimate me based on it, but I use that to my advantage in the kitchen. I can be very demanding."

She knew he was talking about cooking but a part of her was thinking he'd also be demanding in the bedroom. She cleared her throat.

"I am, too," she said. Running the bakery with Alysse was hard work and they'd only become successful by making sure the bakery always came first.

"Cupcake girl—"

"If you call me *cupcake girl* again I'm not going to be so nice."

"This was you being nice?" he asked.

And though the tone was still there in his voice she glanced up at his eyes and saw a hint of a sparkle. She liked him and looked forward to kicking his butt in the kitchen.

"Guess you're not the only one who is more spice than sugar," she said.

The door opened and they were met with a long line of folks waiting to sign in.

"I'm surprised to see so many people here today," she said.

"I'm not. The prize money is going to bring out everyone from executive chefs to prep cooks," he said. "I'm going to wash up. See you in the kitchen."

She watched him walk away before giving herself a mental slap. She wasn't here to repeat the mistakes from her past, but to fix them. This time she was going to do it right and that meant no falling for another chef even if he did have a killer smile, sexy ass and a charming accent.

REMY CRUZEL HAD GROWN up in one of the most famous kitchens in New Orleans. Gastrophile—the three Michelin starred restaurant that raised the bar and set the new standard for American Creole cooking. His grandfather and great-uncle had shocked the culinary world by getting three Michelin stars—something hard to achieve outside of Paris and even harder to do when you weren't French by birth. But the Cruzel brothers had done it and then passed that expertise on to their children.

Everyone quieted down as three men walked into the main room. He recognized Hamilton Ramsfeld, a popular American chef who his father said was a pompous ass who'd lost his love of food in his quest for notoriety. But then his old man was a hard man to impress.

"Hello, chefs, I am the head judge Hamilton Ramsfeld and the other judges in this competition are Lorenz Morelli executive chef and owner of a string of successful high-end Italian restaurants and Pete Gregoria, the publisher of *American Food* magazine."

"We look forward to tasting the dishes you prepare for us," Lorenz said in his heavy Italian accent. "Everyone on the left side of the room will come with me," Lorenz instructed. "Everyone on the right will stay here with Hamilton."

"Good luck to you all," Pete said.

The field of chefs here today was as diverse as he'd expected it to be and he wasn't surprised when the judges immediately divided the room in two.

He saw Cupcake Girl go with the other group and gave her a mock-salute. She was cute and funny but he wasn't here to flirt with women, he was here to prove he had the cooking chops to take over as Chef Patron at Gastrophile in New Orleans. His family name was legend in the food world and it wasn't Stephens. He'd lied on his application.

It was hard to know how much of the praise heaped on his head was due to his last name and how much was due to his skills. So Remy Etienne Cruzel had become Remy Stephens. He didn't know how long he could keep up the ruse, but on his side was the fact that none of the celebrity chefs were friends of his father and Remy had kept a rather low profile at the Culinary Institute of America and while working at Gastrophile.

"Welcome to *Premier Chef—the Professionals* Audition. A love of food has brought you here today but we will only be accepting those of you who have real skill and ability in the kitchen. You might be the king of the kitchen back home, but here in this competition you will have to earn everything. Every new day will bring another chance to prove yourself and at the end of the 12 weeks if you have what it takes you will be the new Premier Chef," head judge Hamilton Ramsfeld said.

Remy nodded knowing this was exactly what he needed to hear.

"Chefs, each of you will prepare a dish from our pantry in 15 minutes that demonstrates your culinary point of view. When the time is up your dish will be judged and only half of your number will make it onto the show."

"Yes, chef," was chorused by the cooks waiting to get in the kitchen. They'd set up a line of tables in a big circle around the room and Remy was anxious to get to his station and start his *mis en place*. He knew what he could cook well in 15 minutes and already he was prepping in his head.

Remy didn't really care who the judges were as long as they scrutinized him for his dishes and not his pedigree, and by lying about who he was he'd ensured they would. They called start and the chefs all ran to the pantry to gather ingredients. It reminded Remy of a game his grandfather used to play with him when he was little. Hiding ingredients in the cupboard and then making him wear a blindfold to see if he could sniff out the items.

He had an image of Cupcake Girl in a blindfold and little else as he directed her around his kitchen back home. He shrugged off that thought and forced his mind back to the competition. It'd be embarrassing if he were sent home before filming even began.

He gathered his ingredients and prepared his dish, cooking easily under the pressure of the clock.

"Dude, this is intense," said the shaggy blond guy next to him. "I'm used to working under the gun but not with this many people around."

"It is crazy, but I think they do that to rattle you," Remy said.

"It's not shaking you," the guy said.

"I've worked under some shouters in my day so it takes more than this to rattle me," Remy said, thinking of his father who didn't let blood temper his tongue when Remy screwed up.

"Me, too. I'm Troy, by the way."

"Remy." He didn't want to chat but needed to get his

dish finished and plated. A quick glance at the clock confirmed that he was right on schedule.

Troy kept up a constant stream as he cooked and Remy had worked with talkers before and had to be honest and admit he didn't like them. The kitchen was for cooking not for talking. He didn't trust a chef who was busy rattling on instead of focusing on his dish.

"Time."

Remy put his hands up and stepped back from his station. The judges came around to taste and he wiped his sweaty hands on his pants, as they tasted his dish. He couldn't remember being this nervous since his first day at the CIA.

"Good. Nice balance of sweet and heat. I like it," Hamilton said.

"Thank you, chef."

The other judges also complimented him. And he realized he was good. He'd known it, but it was nice to hear it from someone else.

They called names of the contestants going home. Troy didn't make the cut and gave Remy a wave as he walked out the door. Remy wasn't surprised. This was a serious competition meant for those who were serious about their work. The other group rejoined them and he noticed Cupcake Girl in the center of the pack.

She was cute with her pixie haircut and her delicate features. Her hair was jet black and her figure petite but curvy. As Hamilton started talking to them again Cupcake Girl's cute ass and the way her jeans fit distracted Remy.

"…teams," Hamilton said.

Dammit. He should have been listening instead of staring at the woman. He had a feeling his sweet tooth was going to be his downfall. "What'd he say?" he asked the man next to him.

"We're going to be put on two person teams and will cook against the other teams, at the end of the round half of us will go home and the remaining chefs will be going onto the show."

"Thanks."

"Come forward and take a knife from the cutting block. There are 15 teams, you will be given a number and A or B. The A knife is the head of the team. You will have thirty minutes to plan your dish and then an hour to execute it."

Everyone moved forward to take a knife and Remy drew 7B. "My lucky number."

"Mine too," a soft feminine voice said from behind him. "And I get to be in charge. My fate has definitely changed since the elevator."

"Cupcake Girl," he said. "I hoped you'd make it through. I think I should be in charge since I'm a trained chef and you are a baker."

"Southern boy, I'm the leader on this mission you can either follow me or perish in flames, but either way I'm not about to screw up a challenge."

He liked her spunky attitude, but he wasn't about to risk going home because of her. He'd let her think she was in charge but no way was he putting his fate in her hands. "What did you have in mind?"

"Well, I'm from LA and you're from the south so I was thinking some kind of taco-po-boy combo. The dishes both have their roots in common street fare. Working class food that we can elevate to fine dining," she said.

"I like the idea. Can you make your own tortillas?" he asked.

"I can," she said with a grin.

"I'll make the filling a shrimp and andouille sausage blend with some vegetables in it."

She nodded. "Sounds good. What do you think of a hint of lime in the tortillas?"

"Yes, that's what we need. But we're still at street food level with this," he said.

She looked over at him with those large chocolate brown eyes of hers. "We can do it three ways and have a plate with three different tacos on it."

He could see that she was here to win but he still wasn't sure she had the cooking skills needed to execute her plan. They discussed the other two tacos and then went into the pantry to gather ingredients. Staci talked to everyone she met and joked. She was easy going and that concerned him.

Could someone so laid back win? He wasn't too sure about trusting her instincts on the dish. He'd seen other chefs going for lamb and beef.

He started working the dish allowing his experience and instincts to take over. He changed a few things from her original suggestion and felt her at his shoulder one time. She reached over and put her finger in his bowl.

"What are you doing?"

"Tasting. It's all about layers. Thought you'd know that, Southern man."

He did know that but he'd been busy trying to make sure he got everything done in the allotted time. She brought her finger to her lips and her small pink tongue darted out to taste the sauce on her finger. He mentally groaned as all thoughts of cooking took a back seat. She was damn sexy and he had the feeling she knew it when she winked at him.

"A little spicy, but then I like things hot," she said, walking back to her station.

He watched her for another second before someone called out that they only had ten minutes left and Remy forced his mind back to the competition and off his sexy competitor. He had to stay focused or everything he wanted to prove would be lost. He only wished that Staci wasn't such a distraction.

2

DESPITE WHAT SHE'D SAID about being in charge, Staci knew that Remy had done some of his own things. But since this was a competition and neither of them wanted to go home, she gave him a pass. Plus, his additions were delicious.

When they started plating their dish, he reached around her to adjust the garnish on the middle taco and his arm brushed hers. Staci took a deep breath, forcing herself to ignore the man and focus on the chef.

"Not bad, but you didn't do what I said."

"I've been cooking a long time, *chère*, I don't necessarily follow instructions."

"If we go home you'll wish you had," she said. "I didn't take a ninety minute bus ride only to be sent home today."

"I'm not planning on going home which is why I simply perfected your idea."

"You're cocky," she said, not at all impressed with his attitude. She tried a bit of the filling left over from the plated dishes. Dammit, it was good. Better than she'd anticipated because she hadn't thought, she sheepishly admitted, that someone who looked like he did could cook.

"Well?" he asked, lifting one eyebrow at her.

"It'll do."

That startled a laugh out of him and she caught her breath as he smiled at her for the first time since they'd met. Really smiled so that his whole face lit up.

"Oh, it will more than do. Let's see if you are up to snuff, *chère*."

She knew the flat bread she made was the best that he'd ever taste. "Angels weep because they can't get my bread in heaven."

He quickly tore off a piece of the bread still on the tray and popped it in his mouth. He chewed slowly and she found herself watching his mouth. She wondered how his lips would feel on hers.

"It'll do."

"I know," she said. She glanced around and noted that the judges were getting closer to their station. They had been directed to stand back from the table until the judges approached them.

Hamilton was the first judge to reach them. He motioned Staci and Remy forward with an arrogant wave of his hand. Staci remained where she was before Remy nudged her with his foot. She hated arrogance in a man. It was okay to be proud of what you accomplished but it was something else entirely for a person to act like such a jerk.

"Your dish looks interesting," Hamilton said. "A little plebian."

"Our taste is anything but," Staci said.

Remy elbowed her. She glared at him.

"Once the camera crew is in place we will ask you about your dish, then taste it," Lorenz said coming over.

The cameraman got into place, a make-up person arrived and brushed something off of Staci's cheek. "What was that?"

"Flour," she said, then with a final whisk of her make-up wand she walked away.

Great, Staci thought, she'd been standing there looking like a messy little girl with flour on her face. She wished she'd known…but then it was a good thing she hadn't. It might have affected how she'd acted toward Remy and Hamilton and she didn't want that. She was serious about her food and this competition and she wanted to let the boys know she'd come to win.

"I think we are ready," the director said. "Go."

"Tell us a little about yourselves," Pete invited them. "Staci, you're a baker?"

"Yes, I co-own a cupcake bakery in San Diego called Sweet Dreams. I was trained at Le Cordon Bleu in Paris."

"And Remy?" Lorenz asked in that sexy Italian accent of his.

"I'm from Nawlins," he said, combining the two words into one with his smooth southern accent. "I learned to cook at my granddad's elbow. I've been working down there but am currently between gigs."

"Staci, you were the leader on this dish, tell us what you prepared for us."

"We combined what makes both of our culinary influences so great. A mixture of street food from the Big Easy and So Cal. Its a trio of po-boy tacos."

"Remy, what did you make?" Hamilton asked as Lorenz cut the first taco into thirds.

"The filling," he said.

"What's in them?" Pete asked.

"Shrimp and andouille, lime crusted tilapia and Portobello mushrooms Vera Cruz style."

"Sounds interesting," Lorenz said. "We are going to taste now."

All three men sampled the tacos and Staci felt her heart in her throat as she waited for them to give their critique. She'd tried the food. She knew that she and Remy had put together a good dish but now she was so nervous. She reached over and grabbed his wrist, as the silence seemed to grow.

Hamilton glanced at Lorenz and than at Pete.

"I really enjoyed this. The mixture of spiciness with the lightness of the bread. Well done," Pete said.

"I liked it too," Lorenz said. "The sausage was delicious and the seasoning layered and complex."

"Well that's three of us who'd come back for more of this. You two worked well together," Hamilton said.

With that the judges moved on, Remy's hand turned in her grasp and he briefly held her hand before dropping it. She wanted to jump up and down but Remy didn't seem to think it was time to celebrate.

"What's the matter? You look almost nervous."

"I'm hardly that. I just don't believe in counting my chickens before they're hatched."

"Um…all three judges liked our food. It's a safe bet that we'll be asked to stay," Staci said.

"I want to hear what he's saying to the others. This is a competition. Just because we made a good dish doesn't mean the other competitors didn't as well," Remy said.

She nodded. And for the first time really looked at the other chefs and the dishes they'd put together. Everyone wanted this chance to make it to the next level. Everyone wanted to win and she had to remember that.

The chefs next to them had made a dry rubbed brisket that they had sliced thin and steamed. "Sounds iffy to me," Staci said. "Brisket needs to be slow cooked."

"I agree, but Pete seems like he's enjoying it."

She had to admit the restaurant critic did seem to be enjoying the meat. But Hamilton made a face and spat his portion back out. "Dry."

"It is dry," Lorenz agreed. "But it's admirable that you tried to do a brisket in the time allotted and I love the spice combination in the rub. Whose recipe is that?"

"Mine," the tall, skinny chef said.

"Good job, Dave. It really flavors the meat and to be honest makes up for the dryness," Lorenz said.

"I enjoyed it," Pete said. "The barbecue sauce you made covers up the lack of moisture in the meat."

"Thanks," Dave said.

The judges finished up their tasting and they were all told to clean up their stations while a final decision was reached. Remy was introspective as he worked quickly and efficiently. She watched him moving and then realized what she was doing.

She always had the worst timing in her infatuations

and it seemed the worst taste in men. She'd let a man ruin her cooking career once. Was she really going to let that happen again?

"Don't worry, *chère*, whatever happens today, you can cook and no one can take that from you," he said. "I enjoyed working with you today."

"Me, too," she said.

They were all told to move back to their stations as a final decision had been reached. Remy stood next to her and this time he squeezed her hand as Hamilton started talking.

"We've sampled some truly fine dishes given that we asked you to work with a chef whose style was different from yours and gave you a time restraint. We know you can all cook; this competition is designed to take you beyond that. Therefore the winners of this challenge and staying in the competition are…

"Staci Rowland and Remy Stephens," Lorenz announced.

Remy tugged her close for a victory hug but he held her a little longer than he should have and when she pulled back there was a new awareness in his eyes.

REMY MADE SURE HE WASN'T in the same Escalade as Staci when they left the studio and were driven to the Premier Chef house in Malibu. They were in a luxury home that overlooked the Pacific.

The water was bluer than his beloved Gulf of Mexico but the scent of salt in the air reminded him of home. There were production assistants in the house when they arrived. And they were all directed where to go in the eight-bedroom house. They'd be sharing two to a room to begin with and the producers had already assigned them into pairs. Remy was in a room overlooking the ocean with Quinn Lyon.

"Dude, do you mind if I take this bed?" Quinn asked.

Remy shrugged. "That's fine. Where are you from?"

"Seattle. I'm the executive chef at Poisson...one guess what our specialty is?"

Remy smiled. There was an easy-going nature about Quinn and he reminded Remy of one of his Cajun uncles who was a shrimper. "Fish, right?"

"Hell, yes. Your accent says you're from the south—where?"

"Nawlins'," he said.

"Where do you work?"

"Currently, I'm between jobs," he said. It was sort of the truth since he'd taken a leave of absence from Gastrophile.

"That's cool. I saw you working today, you keep a neat station," Quinn said.

"I began cooking with my dad and he's a tyrant in the kitchen."

Quinn laughed. "My old man was a logger, didn't know anything about food."

"How'd you come to be a chef?"

"Dropped out of high school," Quinn said. "Started as a dishwasher and worked my way up. I never thought I'd be a chef when I was a kid. I mean, girls cooked where I came from, you know?"

"No, I don't. The women in my family can cook but the kitchen has always been filled with men. I can't remember a time when anyone thought I'd be anything but a chef."

"What's your family think of you being unemployed?" he asked.

"Not too fond of that. But getting on this show will probably help ease their minds," he said. The truth was his parents didn't know where he was right now. But he figured that Remy Stephens's family would be happy that he was cooking with the chance of employment at the end of the show. "What about your family?"

"My wife's great. My dad moved to Alaska so he's not that involved with my day-to-day life," Quinn said. "I don't know if I should unpack or not."

"I am," Remy said. "My *grandmère* is superstitious and she's always said that if you believe you'll succeed you will and vice versa."

"Ah, that's confidence not superstition," Quinn said, unzipping his suitcase and starting to unpack. "But I think you're right. Better to act like I'm here for the long haul."

"Definitely," Remy said.

Quinn had a picture of his wife and one of him with his dad holding up the biggest fish that Remy had ever seen. Quinn kept up a quiet conversation while he moved around the room and Remy learned the other man was thirty-eight and was contemplating an offer to become the chef owner of Poisson. Something he wasn't too sure he wanted to do.

Remy didn't give the other man any advice. He'd learned that decisions that significant had to be made intuitively. Otherwise doubt and resentment followed.

Quinn's cell phone rang and he smiled. "It's the wife."

"I'll leave you alone," offered Remy.

The bedrooms were all on the second floor of the house, which sat, nestled on a cliff overlooking the Pacific ocean. Remy went downstairs and saw that several contestants were on the balcony smoking. But he didn't see Cupcake Girl. He wasn't looking for her, he thought, but part of him knew he was.

She'd been good in the kitchen today and he was happy enough that her direction had resulted in a win, but there could only be one winner of Premier Chef— The Professionals and he needed to be that winner.

His future hinged on it in his mind. He envied Quinn and his easy relationship with his father. The older Lyon hadn't pressured and bullied Quinn into cooking. In his early twenties, Remy would have been happier to make up his own mind and to find his own path. Instead, it had been done for him. Hence his doubts now.

Remy headed toward the kitchen for a bottle of water. Quinn would be tough to beat in any seafood challenge but Remy had grown up on the Gulf so he wasn't too worried, but he wanted to get an idea of what else he was up against.

"You smoke?" a heavily tattooed man with a Jersey accent asked him as he reached the bottom of the stairs.

"No," Remy said.

"Good. So far everyone who's come downstairs is a smoker. I'm Tony. Tony Montea," he said, holding out his hand.

"Remy Stephens," he said shaking the other man's hand. "I'm guessing you're from New York or Jersey."

"Jersey—born and bred. But I work in Manhattan. You'd think I'd cook Italian but my grandmother is French."

"Mine too...well, French Creole," Remy admitted.

"Cool. Did she cook?"

"Yes," he said. "Yours?"

"Yeah. She's the one that taught me to cook. But you can only go so far in a home kitchen," Tony said.

"True. Do you have any formal training?"

"CIA," he said with a smile. "This might be the only place where I don't have to explain that it's the Culinary Institute of America not the Central Intelligence Agency. Though to be honest there are a few from my hood that think I'm with the government."

Remy laughed. "Where do you work?"

"Dans La Jardin," he replied, naming one of the most popular French restaurants in the city.

"Head chef?"

"Nah, junior, but I'm hoping to learn some skills here that will give me a leg up when I get back home."

"Not here to win?" Remy asked.

"Sure I want to win, but I have heard of some of these other chefs," Tony said. "They might be hard to beat."

"They might be," Remy agreed, writing Tony off as a nice guy but not much competition. Anyone who was more concerned about what would happen when he got home versus what needed to happen here wasn't going to win it. And Remy was definitely here to win.

"You're not worried?" Tony asked.

"Nah, but I have been around celebrated chefs before," Remy said.

"Me, too," a tall thin girl with skin the color of cappuccino said, joining them. "I'm Vivian Johns."

"Tony Matea," Tony said. "This is Remy Stephens. Whom have you cooked with?"

"Troy Hudson," Vivian said flashing them both a grin. "I work at The Rib Mart in Austin and he came down there for one of his cook offs."

"How was it?" Remy asked.

"Interesting. He's a solid cook but a lot of his talent gets lost in filming the show. He had a staff with him for the challenge," Vivian said.

"Did you win?" Tony wanted to know.

"Hells to the yeah," she said. "It's hard to beat Austin ribs in Austin but my dish was good. *Really good*. It's interesting how people act around celebrity chefs. Who've you cooked with, Remy?"

"Alain Cruzel," he said. His grandfather was one of the most famous chefs to come out of New Orleans.

"Yeah, I've heard of him. He's one tough guy in the kitchen."

"Yes, he is. He doesn't tolerate mistakes," Remy said. "However, sharing the kitchen with him made me realize even the greatest chefs make mistakes some times. That's why I'm not worried about anyone's reputation."

"You don't have to," Tony said.

"What do you mean?" Remy asked wondering if he'd somehow given away his real name and pedigree.

"You won today. I think that means most of the participants will be gunning for you."

"Not just me," he said. "Cupcake Girl was pretty impressive as well."

"I don't think she's going to take kindly to being called that," Vivian said with a grin.

He didn't think so either but Remy would do whatever he had to in order to avoid the chemistry between them. And to preserve some kind of edge over her. The nickname bothered her so he'd keep using it.

"We need everyone gathered in the living room," the director said.

Everyone moved into the spacious room that had a big screen television on one wall and three long sofas and a number of assorted armchairs casually placed into conversation groups. He saw cupcake girl across the room and forced himself to look away from her.

"The winners of today's challenge are going out to dinner tonight at Martine's where they will have a private tour of the kitchen and talk with their chief sous chef. The rest of you will be participating in a grilling workshop."

Remy shook his head. The last thing he wanted was more time alone with Staci. If he were as superstitious as his grandmother he'd believe that fate was pushing them together.

But he wasn't.

Really.

DINNER ALONE WITH REMY and Chef Ramone wasn't what she'd anticipated when she'd started the day off by spilling tea all over the hottie in the elevator. However, she was happy enough for it now. She got dressed in the one nice dress she'd brought with her.

The instructions for *Premier Chef* were pretty explicit. She'd had to bring her cooking gear but also jeans, a dress, a skirt, a bathing suit and a number of other expected items. Still, it was the specific clothing that had struck her as funny.

She knew it was a television show and that they'd want them all to look a certain way but beyond that she hadn't given what she wore much thought. Now that she was heading to one of the LA areas nicest restaurants she was glad she'd gone shopping with Alysse last weekend.

She enjoyed spending time with the co-owner of Sweet Dreams, especially since Alysse was so busy—engaged to be married and busily determined to expand their cupcake business. Staci had decided to take a break from the day-to-day running of the bakery to get ready for this show. Staci was the first to admit her dreams lay in a different direction now.

The bakery had saved her sanity when she'd first come back to California but that was a long five years ago and given that she was almost thirty, Staci felt it was time to figure out what she wanted from life. And she couldn't until she made up for her past mistakes. Until she resolved her lingering doubts about her abilities as a chef. This show was her chance to do that.

She did a double check of her make-up, although she knew that the production person would re-apply it and make it heavier for the television cameras.

"You look good," her roommate Vivian said.

"Thanks. I wasn't sure that I'd be wearing this dress on TV. Do you think it's too low cut?" she asked. She'd tried it on in the store but had been wearing a sports bra so she hadn't noticed how much cleavage it revealed.

"Not at all. Sex sells, baby. It also distracts. If Remy is staring at your chest it should give you an edge over him."

She sighed inwardly. It was a contest after all. She wanted Remy distracted and off his A game. But at the same time using her body to win, well, why not? Remy hadn't hesitated to use his sexy southern accent to distract her.

She grabbed her handbag and made sure she had her moleskin recipe journal in there. The journal had seen better days and was bulging with pages and photos she'd added. She never went anywhere without the journal. She liked to make notes about the meals she ate and she found eating out always inspired her palate.

"Knock 'em dead," Vivian said.

"I hope so," Staci replied as she left their room. She was used to living alone, cooking alone and spending most of her time by herself, so this living with the other contestants could be a strain.

Remy was waiting in the foyer with Jack, the director and one of the producers. She almost missed a step on the stairs staring at Remy. His thick black hair was slicked back. He wore a white dress shirt left casually open at the neck and a navy dinner jacket and gray pants. He glanced at his watch and then at the stairs, his mouth dropping open when he saw her.

She gave herself a mental high five and forced herself to smile at him in what she hoped was a casual way. To be honest, he was oozing sexiness in his dinner wear, so she wasn't entirely sure what impression she gave off.

"Now that you are both here we will head over to the restaurant. We won't be filming until we are there so you can relax."

"Thanks," Remy said. "Will we be driving ourselves?"

"No. We have a production assistant who will take you and pick you up. During the course of the show you will always be in our hands. Chef Ramone doesn't like cell phones and he has requested you leave them with us."

"Okay," Staci said, opening her handbag to retrieve her phone, which she handed to Jack.

"What's that book in your bag?" the producer asked.

"Just my food journal. I like to write down the meals I eat."

"I'm sure that will be fine. Though we will check with the chef before you arrive and if it's not, you'll have to give it to one of our staff at the location."

She didn't like the thought of letting anyone else have her journal but she wasn't going to argue about it right now. Jack directed them out the door and into a Mercedes sedan.

"How many vehicles do you have?" Remy asked.

"Enough. In this case Mercedes is sponsoring one of the upcoming challenges and giving away this car as a prize."

"Nice. I hope I win," Staci said. "I've been riding the bus for too long."

Remy laughed. "Ah, without the bus I wouldn't have that great first impression of you."

She shook her head remembering how she'd landed in his arms. "I could have done without that."

Soon they were both seated in the backseat and being whisked across town toward the famous restaurant. Instead of thinking about the evening or even the contest, Staci's thoughts hadn't drifted any further than the man sitting next to her.

She wished she'd made a better first impression on him but she knew that her skills in the kitchen had made up for her stumble. And if she were honest, she wouldn't trade their first meeting for anything.

"Nervous?" he asked.

"A little. But not really," she said. "You?"

"No. I'm curious to see his techniques. I haven't cooked much outside of the South."

"I was trained in Paris," she said.

"Really? Pastry?" he asked.

"Yes and everything else," she admitted.

"Then why are you the co-owner of a cupcake bakery? You should be working in the finest kitchens in the world."

"That is a long story," she said.

"Well, we do have a long drive ahead of us," he replied.

3

THE WARMTH OF THE CAR'S interior felt like an intimate cocoon and it would have been easy for her to forget that Remy was her competitor. Yet, this situation was so far removed from what she knew life to be like. Remy might be an out-of-work chef but he was clearly used to luxury. He sat relaxed next to her in his expensive clothes.

What was his story? Did she want to know? A lot of people said it was better to know your enemy but given her personality flaw regarding men, she thought a little mystery was probably in order.

"You were going to tell me how a Cordon Bleu chef ends up owning a cupcake bakery," he said in that sultry southern way of his.

It would be easy to dismiss him as an innocent were it not for the shrewd look in his eyes. She didn't have to guess to know that he was one of those who subscribed to the know-your-enemy theory.

"Was I?" she asked, turning toward him. The fabric of her skirt slid up her legs and she waited to see if he had noticed.

He had. But he arched one eyebrow at her to let her know that he knew she'd done it deliberately. She shrugged and he smiled.

"It's clear that neither of us is going to forget this is a competition," he said.

"I'm here to win," she said. "I have to assume you are too."

"Indeed. Why else would I travel across the country with just my knives and culinary training?"

"Where did you train?" she asked, turning the tables back to him.

"CIA. But we'll learn about that during the competition. I want to know more about you. The things you aren't going to reveal in front of the camera," he said, as he shifted to stretch his arm along the back of the seat. His fingers just inches from her shoulder, she felt the heat of his body against her skin.

"But those facts aren't ones I'll give up for nothing. What are you going to offer me in return, what secrets do you keep, Southern Man?"

She realized that the attraction ran both ways and that Remy wasn't afraid to turn the tables on her. She cleared her throat.

"Show me yours and I'll show you mine," he said.

"That hardly seems fair unless I know what you're offering to give up," she said.

"Okay, tell me how you got started cooking. Where did your culinary journey begin?" he asked, running his finger along the side of her cheek.

She turned her face away from his touch. "And you'll do the same?"

"Oui, *chère*," he said.

She rubbed one finger along his beard-stubbled jaw just to try to keep him off-balance and because she was longing to know what it felt like. He seemed to just reach out and touch her whenever he wanted to.

"Good. I grew up in here in southern California. I'm an only child and was always in the kitchen with my grandmother who practically raised me," she said. "Your turn."

"I grew up in Louisiana. Though I live and work in New Orleans now, I spent a lot of time in the bayou as a young boy with my grandmother's people. I learned to shrimp and cook off of what we found each day. I didn't realize how great a gift that would be as a chef."

"I bet. My grandmother used to buy whatever was on sale at the grocery store when we went. She never had a menu and when we'd get home she'd combine the ingredients in different ways."

"Sounds like we are similar in our upbringing," he said.

"Maybe. You seem very comfortable surrounded by luxury," she said.

"Do I?"

"Yes. This is probably the nicest car I've been in unless you count the limo I took to prom. I don't think that's the case with you."

He laughed. "Who did you go to prom with?"

"A boy who thought he loved me," she said.

"Why did the boy think he loved you?" Remy asked.

She was not about to start talking about her rocky

past and the loves that might have been. "Don't avoid the question."

"What was the question?"

She frowned at him. "You're difficult and cagey. What exactly are you hiding, Remy Stephens?"

"I believe that some things shouldn't be spoken of. But you are right, I did grow up in a comfortable home financially. However, that's not as interesting as a boy who thought he loved you. Didn't you love him?"

"I'm not talking about that," she said. She hadn't allowed herself to really care about anyone when she'd been younger because she'd had big dreams of leaving California and going to Paris. She was going to be the next Julia Child.

"What about emotionally? Was your home as comfortable in that way as it was financially?" she asked. She'd met more than one person who hid behind evasion and had grown up in a difficult home. Having money didn't always mean that someone had an easy upbringing.

"It was good. My family are all Cajun or French so there is a lot of passion and tempers flaring, but I always knew I was loved." His voice revealed the truth of those words. And she thought about how he'd been in the kitchen. There was something very controlled about Remy. She doubted he'd be the sort of man who'd let passion for a woman interfere with his desire to win.

She needed to remember that.

"Spoiled?" she asked.

"A little. But I can't blame my parents for that. I just like to get my way," he said.

"Like you did in the competition this afternoon. Doing what you thought was best instead of what I told you."

He shrugged again. "I have to give my all in the kitchen. Even if that means making other chefs mad."

"Is that why you are between gigs right now? Do you have a hard time taking orders?" she asked.

He rubbed the bridge of his nose and pulled his arm off the back of the seat to his lap. She guessed that she'd asked a question that cut too close to whatever he was hiding from her. Whatever his emotional vulnerable point was. *Interesting.*

"Perhaps," he said. "Mostly it's that I have been praised for my cooking but by those who've known me my entire life. I want to know if I'm really good."

"Why? Did something happen to shake your confidence?" she asked.

"Did something happen to you?" he asked, focusing that intense blue gaze of his on her. "I bet it did. No one goes from Paris to a cupcake bakery without a big event forcing the change."

"True. I guess we both have our secrets," she said. "But I will tell you this, I've never doubted my ability to put a good dish on the table. I know when I'm done cooking that the person eating my food is going to be blown away."

"Do you?"

"Yes. I think you must be the same," she said. "Otherwise why would you come here?"

"Why indeed," he said.

She leaned back against the leather seat and looked

out the window again. This time the answers she sought had nothing to do with her, but with him. "You want external praise."

"Don't you?" he asked.

"I guess. Really I want a chance to get back what I once had," she said, speaking from the heart.

As much as the success she'd had with Sweet Dreams validated her as a chef and businesswoman, she wanted to know that she had the chops to go head-to-head with the best cooks in the world. She'd competed years ago to get that original role in the kitchen of a top Parisian chef, and then she'd thrown it away for love. No, that wasn't right. There hadn't been love between them, but there had been passion and danger, she thought. It had been very dangerous to give in to her passions.

Yes. That was what had been missing from her life. That was what she was afraid she'd never find again. Her passions for living and for cooking. It was only when she embraced both, that she really did have balance. Yet that was the very thing that frightened her the most.

"You look like you just solved the problems of the world," he said.

"Nah, just the problems of one woman. It's funny how you find answers when you didn't know there was a question," she said.

"What did you figure out, *ma chère*?" he asked, lifting his arm against the back of the seat again and touching the side of her face.

No way was she sharing the truth with him, but she knew that if she were going to reclaim her passion in the kitchen she'd have to reclaim it in her life as well.

She needed to figure out a way to balance her personal passions with her professional ones and a part of her felt like maybe she could do that with Remy. But another part of her warned that the last time she'd attempted this she'd been burned. Could she survive another dance of passion with a chef?

REMY HAD COME TO COOK but he found most of his time so far had been taken up with thinking about the sexy little woman seated next to him. Her perfume was elusive but tempting, and he found the scent distracting as they worked next to Chef Ramone in the kitchen. Remy shook his head, forcing his attention back to the cutting board in front of him. The executive chef moved off to take care of an emergency on the other side of the kitchen and Staci moved closer to Remy.

"He's so low-key I almost don't believe he could prepare these spectacular dishes."

"I know what you mean. I've never met a chef who doesn't yell," Remy said. "Certainly never worked with one who didn't."

"Me either. Even Alysse and I yell back and forth at the bakery."

"That's your partner?" he asked.

"Yes. She's funny. Usually we're just telling each other stories from the night before or I'm bossing her around," Staci said.

"Do you do that a lot?" he asked. He'd finished dicing the vegetables he'd been assigned to work with by the chef. Staci still had half her pile to go. He reached over and took the carrots from her.

She smiled her thanks. "Yes, I do boss her around a lot. But not just her, anyone who needs my advice."

"Do I need it?"

"I don't know. A part of me wants to say yes, but I don't know you well enough. You're wicked with that knife."

"Knife skills are one of the best weapons in a chef's arsenal," he said.

"Yes, they are, Remy," Chef Ramone said returning to them.

"You've done well with the task I assigned you. Ready to assemble our dish?"

Remy found the same comfort of working in the kitchen with Staci and Chef Ramone as he did working in his own kitchen back home. It was telling he thought that this was home for him even though he was thousands of miles from New Orleans.

And he wasn't sure he could find his own way. Staci messed with his concentration and that intrigued him. He'd had affairs before, he was too passionate and his sexual drive too high for him not to. But he'd never allowed himself an affair with another chef. It seemed to him that life was best served by keeping his personal and professional lives separate.

Now, he wasn't sure. He watched her dip her spoon into the sauce she was preparing and stared at her full lips and saw her eyes sparkle. He suppressed a groan. In his mind he moved closer and leaned in to taste the sauce but not from the spoon, from her.

"Want a lick?" she asked.

He snapped back to the present and nodded. He

wanted way more than a lick but that would be a good place to start. She held the spoon out to him, but instead of taking it from her hand, he wrapped his hand around her wrist and drew her to him.

He brought their hands up and then he leaned down to run his tongue over the sauce, keeping eye contact with her the entire time. Her lips parted and her tongue darted out again, just as it had before. Her pupils dilated and there was a rosy flush that climbed up her face.

"Delicious," he said, letting his hand drop and stepping back to his station.

"Thanks," she said, her voice thready, husky even and he knew that in the game of flirtation, he'd just won the round.

It was at that moment that he knew he wasn't leaving California without taking Staci Rowland to his bed. He'd thought that she'd distract him from cooking but he was coming to realize that if he didn't have her, it would be more of a distraction.

She was temptation incarnate and he was from The Big Easy. He'd been raised to indulge his passions in the kitchen and out and even though this would be the first time that he combined the two, he found the anticipation exquisite.

"Remy?" she asked.

He glanced over at her and saw the confusion in her eyes. And for a second he wondered if he'd misjudged her but then she licked her lips again and he smiled. He knew that he hadn't.

Staci seemed as if she were dealing with some issues in this competition, much like the rest of them.

And though tonight it was just the two of them, he knew that whatever knowledge he gleaned about her would be useful for the rest of the weeks ahead.

He closed the gap between them. Put his hands on her shoulders and leaned down as he drew her closer. He brushed his lips over hers and tasted the buttery sweetness of the sauce but also the indescribable taste of Staci. It was unique, mysterious and so addictive he didn't want to stop kissing her.

Yet he knew he had to. He stepped back and saw her watching him with an unfathomable expression. He'd shocked her. Hell, he'd surprised himself because he'd thought the young impulsive man he'd been was gone forever. But he was glad that he was back.

He thought he needed to be a little impulsive if he was going to find the right path forward for himself and for Gastrophile.

He had an idea of a seasoning to add to the dish and turned away from Staci and returned to his station. Cooking with renewed enthusiasm, when he was done and they both presented their dishes to the chef, he knew he'd prepared something different.

Something unique and something that he couldn't have come up with if he hadn't kissed Staci. It was as if she were a muse.

She was quiet and stole sideways looks at him, but he didn't face her. He waited for the verdict on the dishes, unsurprised when his was pronounced the winner.

He felt a balm of satisfaction and realized that he owed Staci a big thank you, but more than that he wanted to keep cooking with her by his side. Earlier today he'd been resentful of having to listen to someone else in the kitchen but tonight he acknowledged that only with outside input could he move to the next level.

Chef Ramone stepped away again and Staci put her hands on her waist as she turned to him. "What was that about?"

"What?"

"Kissing me like that. I thought we were both professionals," she said.

"We are," he admitted. "That kiss had nothing to do with our cooking and everything to do with the fire burning between us. I thought it would be distracting…"

"Wasn't it?" she asked. "It was for me."

"No," he said. "It wasn't distracting. It was inspiring." He leaned over and kissed her again. "Thank you for that."

She semi-glared at him and he felt her displeasure. "You're welcome, I guess. I don't want you doing that again."

"I'm not making any promises," he said.

STACI KEPT HER DISTANCE from Remy for the ride home. She'd thought flirting with him would give her an edge and it had surprised her how easily he'd flipped the tactic on her. But as she watched him moving easily around the living room of the house and talking to the other competitors she knew there was more to it than that.

There was something about Remy that was shaking her to her core. She had to tread carefully. Where kissing her had spurred him and inspired him to make a creative and unique dish, it had floored her and made her put up something mediocre. She was lucky that tonight hadn't been a judged cooking session that counted. She was lucky that it had merely been a learning experience. She wasn't going to forget it either.

"How was it?" Vivian asked, coming up next to her and handing her a glass of wine.

Staci took a swallow of the dry white wine as she weighed what to say to Viv. They were roommates so the impulse to share what had happened was strong, but she also knew from watching these kinds of reality television shows that close personal relationships often backfired. Even friendships.

"It was fantastic," she said. She also knew that she wasn't going to ever say anything negative about anything.

"I knew it. I'm going to win the next challenge," Vivian said.

"Are you?"

"Hell, yes. I wouldn't mind being whisked away for a private dinner with dreamy Remy."

"He might not be the runner up," Staci warned.

"Why? Did he show you some weaknesses tonight?" Vivian asked.

No, she thought. She'd shown herself some weaknesses and she knew that she had to figure out how to turn that into a strength. She could do it. She just had to remember…what? She had no idea how to handle Remy and she knew it.

She'd known it from the moment she'd crashed into his arms in the elevator. He rattled her and she'd thought that by being her usual bold self she could gain the upper hand, but he'd turned that against her. How had he known that would work? But she thought maybe he hadn't known for sure and had only chanced upon…wait, a second, she thought. He didn't realize he'd thrown her. He'd been too engrossed in what had been going on with himself.

She had to remember how her grandmother had admonished her many times when she'd been growing up. Not everything was about her.

"So?"

"Sorry, Viv. He's a great chef and it's going to take a lot of skill to beat him," she said. "He took the chef's dish and made it taste even better. You know that's saying a lot."

"Dang. Well, I will tell you that Dan doesn't have any butchering skills. He made a mess of the fish tonight. He couldn't get a steak out of a salmon. I mean that's first year skills, right?" Vivian asked.

"Yes, it is. But he did make that rub that Lorenz liked. We might have to watch out for his flavors."

"True. I'm ready for the individual challenges but the team ones worry me," she admitted.

"Me, too," Staci said. "I hate having to depend on anyone other than myself."

They chatted a while longer about the competition until slowly everyone got ready for bed. Vivian put in her iPod headphones and switched off her light. She drifted off to sleep a little after midnight, but Staci was still wide awake.

Questions ran through her head and images of the dishes she'd eaten that night flashed through her mind.

She took her journal and got out of bed. Pulling on a sweatshirt, she then walked through the quiet house to the deck that overlooked the ocean. The moon was full, lending some light to the evening and she sat down on one of the padded deck chairs, letting the soothing sound of the ocean ease her confusion.

She opened her notebook and started writing about what she'd eaten and cooked that night. She wasn't too surprised to see that Remy featured in her notes. She focused on him, finding the part that made sense and the many things that didn't. Her sauce had been her downfall. Kissing him…no, that had been the thing that had knocked her off her game. Until that moment she'd been fine.

She'd teased him and it had backfired. But only because she hadn't been prepared for him to be as bold as she had been. And that had been a mistake she wouldn't make again.

"Can I join you?"

She glanced around to see Remy standing in the doorway. He wore a pair of faded jeans and a long sleeved black t-shirt that molded his upper body. He held a mug in his hand and had bare feet.

She nodded and gestured toward the chair next to her.

He sat down, leaning against the back of the lounge chair and saying nothing for a long minute or two. He sipped his hot drink and she felt that he was toying with her, but when she looked over at him she saw he wasn't.

Not everything is about you, she reminded herself again.

"Why can't you sleep?" she asked.

"Quinn snores," he said. "But I'm too restless from cooking tonight. If I was home I'd be in the kitchen trying all the different dishes that are in my head."

"Same here. It was inspiring to see what Chef Ramone had done. I mean he started from really humble roots."

"Yes, he did. My grandfather says all good cooking comes from the heart," Remy said.

"Was that what inspired you tonight? I've never tasted that combination of spices before."

He shrugged and took another sip from his mug. "I think I was inspired by something a little lower than my heart."

That startled her and she stared across the space between them trying to ascertain if he was telling the truth or not. And she saw in his eyes that he was. He wanted her.

She put down her notebook, stood up and moved over to sit facing him.

"Are you trying to say that your groin inspired the dish?" she asked, putting her hands against the back of the chair on either side of his face.

"Yes, I am. There was something fiery in that kiss I stole from you," he said. "My dish was a pale imitation of it." He leaned up, tunneling his fingers through her hair and drawing her head down to his and this time when their lips met, she opened her mouth over his, running her tongue along the seam of his lips before thrusting it teasingly into his mouth.

He moaned, angling his head to the right to deepen their kiss. His hands slid down her shoulders to her waist and he drew her closer to him. She straddled his lap, tried to taste more of him. God, he was addicting.

And addictions seldom were a good thing, she tried to remind herself but for the moment, logic wasn't in control and she wanted more of the passion Remy inspired.

4

A HOT WOMAN IN HIS LAP wasn't what he'd anticipated tonight but to be honest there was nothing he wanted more. He was high on the exhilaration of the dish he'd created. He felt as if everything inside of him had been pushing toward this interlude. He didn't have all the answers he'd been seeking but thanks in part to Staci he'd found a few of them.

Sliding his arms up and down her back, she shifted to accommodate him, her hands still framing his face. Her fingers were delicate and cool against his beard-stubbled chin; he rubbed his face against her hands breaking the contact with her mouth.

She exhaled a long drawn out sigh as she shifted her weight to settle back on her ankles.

"What am I going to do with you?" she asked.

But he could tell she wasn't really expecting an answer from him. It was more of a question that he'd bet she wasn't even aware she'd muttered out loud. He smoothed his hands over her back, she felt so ethereal in his arms. Like the fairies his little sister collected when they'd been children. Staci didn't belong in this world, yet there was something very real about her.

He felt like the wrong move would send her skittering back into the house and into a permanent retreat.

He wasn't much for being tentative. It went against his hot-blooded Cajun nature. But he was willing to do what was necessary to keep Staci here tonight. He needed her. He wasn't sure how or why but he knew that she'd inspired him tonight and he wanted to keep that energy going.

"Kiss me again," he said as the breeze off the Pacific stirred around them.

She tipped her head to the side. "You'd like that, wouldn't you?"

"Hell, yes, I'm a guy after all."

She smiled at him but the expression didn't reach her eyes and he sensed there was a feeling of sadness in her. He remembered the boy she'd mentioned who'd believed he'd been in love with her.

Remy wanted to know more about Staci. He needed to, yet at the same time he recognized that if he was going to win, and prove to himself what needed proving, he couldn't let her be the first one to make him back down from a challenge.

Yet that very action was impossible. There had been other women in his life but none of them had ever inspired him to cook the way he had tonight. There was no denying it. He could only hope that he'd be able to control his need for Staci. He knew that men who played with fire did get burned.

"But you'd also like it because we're competitors and

you saw the way that you threw me in the kitchen tonight," she said.

He didn't have to feign surprise. He genuinely had
no idea that their embrace had rattled her. But now that
he did, he filed that information away for later. "No, I
didn't."

"Truly?" she asked, tracing her fingers along his five
o'clock shadow.

He closed his eyes and tipped his head to the side
enjoying her touch as sensation spread throughout his
body. His blood seemed to flow heavier in his veins
before pooling between his legs. His erection hardened
and he almost canted his hips forward.

"Yes. I was inspired by our kiss. There was something so hot in that embrace with you I thought I'd explode right there in Chef Ramone's kitchen but then I
channeled it into the dish…I've never done that before.
I always cook from a place of history. Dishes made the
way they've always been made."

"Why?" she asked, running her hands down his
neck and over his shoulders and warmth started to flow
through him. Not unlike what he'd felt earlier in Ramone's kitchen. This woman—Staci—made him feel
things that he knew would complement their situation.
He should put her from his lap and walk away…but he
knew he wasn't going to do that.

He took her wrist and drew her hand lower, rubbing
it over his chest and pectorals. Her hands were small
and petite as she was. Staci called to the wildness in
his soul and he was powerless to ignore it. He wanted

her, but more than that, he wanted to be the man who chased the shadows from her eyes.

She stretched her fingers out and then he felt the bite of her nails through the fabric of his shirt.

He reached around her, she was as hot as the spiciest pepper in his garden and one taste was simply not enough.

He held her hips, bringing her down into contact with his erection. She sighed. The sound of his name on her lips made him shudder. He liked it. He wanted to hear it again when she was breathy and on the cusp of pleasure.

He thrust up against her as her fingers continued to caress him. How he wanted this woman.

Tonight, with only the moon and the sea as his witnesses, he felt free to give in to his desires. He needed to claim her—his muse. He tangled one hand in her short hair and drew her mouth back to his. Her kisses were addictive and he was hungry for more of them. He rubbed his lips over hers until her mouth parted and he slipped his tongue inside her mouth. He was desperate to find that elusive taste that had so intrigued him earlier.

She shifted again, her tongue toying with his. He couldn't get enough of her. He wondered if she'd be both his savior and his downfall. But pushed the thought aside. Only a fool dwelled on thoughts when he had a woman like Staci in his arms.

For tonight she was a gift sent from the gods to inspire him and there was no step he could take that would be out of line. She was his, he thought. Just another element of the new knowledge he had gained on the first step of his journey.

He found the hem of her shirt and slid his hands underneath and up her back. She wasn't wearing a bra, which made him even harder than he already was. Her skin was so smooth he just kept stroking her as he devoured her mouth. She was rocking on his lap, her own hands finding the hem of his shirt and pushing it up under his armpits.

The first brush of her fingers against his bare skin made him burn for more. He pushed her shirt up and she lifted her mouth from his, staring down at him. She pulled her shirt up and off tossing it on the ground next to their chair. He did the same with his shirt and adjusted her on the lounge chair so that he could pull her closer to him. Her center was nestled close to his groin, the tips of her firm breasts brushed against his chest.

Her nipples were hard and pointed, pushing against him and he kept his hand on her back right between her shoulder blades so that he could enjoy that feeling. She lifted her head toward his and her hands were on his face again, pulling him down until their mouths met.

The kiss this time was blatantly carnal and he wanted it to never end. He let his hands explore her body the way his tongue did her mouth. Slowly, with long languid sweeps. It felt as if they had all the time in the world. As if this moment would last forever.

He brought one hand to her backside and urged her to brush her pelvis against him. She did. The slow movement echoed their tongues. He felt a feathering of sensation down his back, surprised at how quickly she was getting to him. He hadn't felt this near to the edge from a little petting since he'd been a randy teenager.

She rubbed her breasts against his chest and he brought his hand from her back around to cup her and tease her nipple with his thumb. She gripped the back of his head, pressing her mouth passionately, fervently to his.

Her hips started to move more rapidly on him and he knew she was on the cusp of orgasm. He scraped his nail around her areola and felt the goose bumps spread, then suddenly she stilled.

She jerked her hips forward and he grabbed her butt as he lifted his hips and held her, his erection right against her center, until she groaned. He was sure she came as she collapsed against his chest, resting her head on his shoulder.

He hugged her in his arms, wanting more but happy for this moment just to hold her. To pretend that he'd captured his muse and that she'd never leave him. His senses were alive as he stroked her hair and whispered softly into her ear.

STACI FELT TOO LANGUID to move and yet she still wanted more. That orgasm had been nice but nothing would truly satisfy her until she felt his hard, hot length inside of her. His hand rested on the crown of her head, her back, then her waist. His fingers dipped beneath the waistband of her pajama pants.

She rubbed his chest, tracing the line of hair that tapered slowly down his midriff disappearing beneath the waistband of his jeans. She mirrored his movement, her fingers beneath his waistband and felt the tip of his erection.

"I'm guessing you liked that."

"Not as much as you did," he said with a wicked grin. "But yes, I definitely liked it."

She shifted around on his lap until she could undo his jeans. He shifted his hips and his cock was thrusting up at her. She wrapped her hand around him and began stroking from root to tip. He shivered and she tightened her grip.

He ran his hands over her torso and rekindled the fires that had been merely banked but not extinguished by her first orgasm. He cupped both of her breasts but she kept her grip in place, moving so that he could touch her the way she liked it.

She extended her shoulders back and watched as he leaned forward. She felt the warmth of his breath against her skin, then the sweep of his tongue. He circled her nipple once, twice, closed his mouth over her and suckled her deeply.

She stroked him slowly, then sped up until she felt his hips lift toward her in counterpoint to her hand. He groaned and his mouth left her breast. He held the back of her neck and brought her mouth to his this time his tongue thrusting so deeply into her that she thought they'd be joined together forever.

He tugged at the fabric of her pajama pants and she slipped them down her thighs and stepped free of them. Immediately, his hands were there on her hips, drawing her down against his cock. She didn't remove her hand except to enable the tip of his erection to enter her. Just the tip as she kept that tight grip on his shaft.

"Put me inside of you."

"You are," she said.

"All of me."

She accommodated him and he muttered a Cajun curse under his breath. She smiled to herself, reveling in both the feel of him and at her power over him. But then he lifted his head and teased her nipple in his mouth again, and she shuddered.

The time for playing the little game she'd been indulging in was over.

She leaned down and whispered dark, intimate words in his ear. Telling him how exquisite he felt and how much she loved what he was doing to her. A second later he filled her completely.

She rocked her pelvis forward trying to take him deeper but he was already as deep as he could go. His hands found her bare buttocks and he rocked her forward. God, she loved the feel of those big hands against her ass. He parted her cheeks and she felt one finger sliding along her furrow and she squirmed closer to him.

Every ounce of her being craved more of his touch. His mouth slid from hers, nibbling down her neck and tempting her without restraint. She shivered as she'd done before and felt everything in her reaching once again toward a climax. But she didn't want it to happen too soon. She wanted this to last as long as it could.

The roughness his stubbled jaw against her cheek tipped her closer to the edge. She dug her fingernails into his shoulders as she rocked her hips harder against his and when he called out her name, she melted. Her orgasm rushed over her as she continued thrusting forward.

His hips moved in sync with her, then she felt him stiffen and eventually relax. Over and over he whispered her name. She, in turn, couldn't stop pressing against him, as she nursed her second orgasm.

Softly panting, his breathing tingled over her sensitized nerves as she fell forward. He wrapped one arm around her shoulder and the other around her waist. She shivered now from the cold and he reached down to grab his shirt, which he draped over her.

She didn't want to move or to face him at this moment. She wanted to pretend that nothing had changed and she'd still be able to view him as just another competitor. And she almost had herself convinced about doing just that until he kissed her gently on the forehead.

That sweet gesture should have meant nothing, instead it made her heart beat faster and there was a hope that maybe this was more than mere lust. She didn't want it to be. Embracing her passion was one thing but falling in love with a competitor would be a disaster and a mistake.

One she wasn't willing to make. She shifted out of his arms and off his lap. She pulled her pajama pants on and tossed his shirt at him while she put hers back on.

"Um…I'm on the pill, not that you asked, but we should be covered."

He nodded as he fastened his jeans and stood up next to her. "I wasn't thinking about anything but you."

His words brought out goosebumps on her arms, but she steeled her heart against them. It was almost as if he knew the exact right words. To make her forget. To distract her. He was playing her.

And she'd have no one but herself to blame if she didn't heed this warning and walk away.

REMY WATCHED HER WALK away knowing that Staci thought this had been a mistake. He rubbed his hand over his face and didn't follow her into the house.

"Am I supposed to say I'm sorry?"

"No," she said, glancing over her shoulder at him. "I should know better."

"Better than what?" he asked. Regret came hard to him and he didn't want to apologize even though he knew he should. He'd taken her because he wanted to, and she wanted him to. And yes, he'd tasted something new and inspiring in her passion, but he'd also hurt her. Something he'd never wanted to happen.

"*You* kissed *me*," he pointed out softly.

"I know," she said. "I don't regret it. I'm mad at myself. I keep making the same mistakes."

"Like what?"

She shook her head. "I think you've seen me naked enough tonight."

She headed into the house and this time he could only watch her go. What had she meant by that? He would figure it out another time. Tonight he had his hands full figuring himself out. At the balcony railing, he pulled his shirt on. He'd always had a clear-cut path in front of him until last year when he'd overheard a restaurant critic saying that this latest generation of Cruzels were slackers.

That one comment had shaken his confidence and made it seem as if he'd taken everything for granted.

Now he was here and tonight he'd felt a little like his old self again but at what cost, he thought. His new confidence had been earned at the expense of Staci. She was battling her own demons, he knew that, but he still didn't like the way that feeling sat on his shoulders. He was in part to blame for what was going on with her.

And he truly didn't want that. More than anything he needed some advice. Despite the late hour, he went inside and came across Dan in the main living room.

"I thought I was the only one up at this time of night," Dan said.

Remy felt lucky that Dan hadn't come up earlier when he'd had Staci in his arms. He shouldn't have been surprised that he hadn't thought of getting caught when he'd had her. All he'd been able to think about was Staci.

"Seems a lot of us are having trouble sleeping tonight," Remy said.

"Yeah." Dan rubbed the back of his neck. "I was the last one to make it in today…I'm excited and nervous about tomorrow."

Remy nodded. That was exactly the way he felt. Each new phase was going to challenge a preconceived notion he had of himself in the kitchen. While he looked forward to finding out what he was made of another part of him worried that he'd made another mistake.

Sleeping with Staci had been a colossal one. He didn't want her to have the impression that he was the type of man who'd use someone to get what he wanted.

"You? The judges practically wept when they tasted your dish," Dan remarked.

"Not quite. Besides that was a team challenge. What will they think of a dish I make on my own?"

"Are you really nervous?" Dan asked.

"No. A little. To be honest, tonight at Chef Ramone's I made a dish that was probably one of the best I've ever prepared. Not sure I can keep up that standard. There are a lot of good chefs here."

Dan smiled. "I can't work as well as I thought I could under pressure. I mean in my own kitchen I can work a dinner service like a pro but going up against the clock and preparing something new…that kind of threw me off," he said.

Remy relaxed as he talked cooking with Dan. It was then that he realized that the guilt he felt at Staci's re-action earlier was easing, too. He hadn't been manipu-lating her. Twice now she'd initiated something sexual with him and twice he'd been blown away by his own reaction to her.

Remy studied the other chef. Dan was younger than him, probably in his mid twenties. "Don't think about it too much. When we get to the kitchens tomorrow just be cool and imagine you're preparing a meal for some-one you love."

"Good idea. But what if the ingredients are weird."

"They probably will be. But it's your knife skills you should be thinking about."

"You heard about that?" Dan asked. "I never went to cooking school. Just learned from working in the kitchens."

"That's no big deal. Just understand your weaknesses. Everyone who goes up against you will be thinking they can butcher better than you can. If it were me, I'd be in the kitchen every second working on them."

"Can you show me how to cut a fish up?" Dan asked.

"Yes," Remy said. "Want to do it now? The fridge is stocked with everything."

"Okay," Dan agreed. "Uh, Remy, why are you willing to help me?"

"Because you're a good chef I'd hate to beat you on a technicality."

Dan laughed and followed Remy to the kitchen. Remy glanced up the stairs to where the bedrooms were and an image of Staci naked invaded his mind. He tried to conjure her curled up under her blankets. He knew she wasn't sleeping and he felt bad about that. She'd invigorated him tonight. He wanted to give her back something. But time would tell what that would be.

He spent the next hour showing Dan the proper way to debone a fish and how to cut it into steaks. The younger man was an attentive student and Remy knew he'd made the right decision to help him out. Two hours later he headed up to his bedroom, smelling of fish, and went straight to the shower. Staci's scent lingered on his skin, too, and he couldn't get the image of her in his arms out of his head.

It wasn't until the water ran cold that he groaned, turned off the shower and dried himself. Eventually, he drifted off to sleep only to be plagued by images of himself in his father's kitchen trying to prepare a dish that would please his father while a naked Staci kept stealing his attention. He woke up in a state of frustration. He hoped the day would bring another new revelation in the kitchen but his dreams had showed him what he already knew.

His doubts and fears were still firmly rooted inside of him and no matter what he discovered here about himself, until he figured out how to accept his own capabilities he'd never find peace.

The odd thing was that in his head his peace was now tied somehow with Staci. It was a mess. She was the last one who'd help him out after last night and to be honest he couldn't blame her. What had felt so right under the moonlight didn't seem very smart in the bright sunlight of morning.

5

STACI WANTED TO FALL right to sleep but she couldn't with all that was on her mind. She'd come here for a very specific reason and tonight it seemed clear that she was capable of letting herself be distracted. What was wrong with her?

Part of her knew it was because she'd never had a positive male role model. She didn't need her shrink to tell her that when she met powerful men she was always drawn to them. And it seemed the more power they had over her dreams and her future the more lethal her attraction was.

But Remy…he had no real power over her other than the attraction. She pulled her cell phone from her bag and texted Alysse. She knew the other woman would be awake and was probably in her kitchen baking because Alysse's fiancé Jay was on an assignment. The retired marine worked for a private security company. And while most of his jobs kept him in the Los Angeles area, he'd recently accepted an assignment in D.C. that had him away from home.

Staci: Can you talk?

Alysse: Yes. Give me a sec. Brownies going in the oven now.

Staci: Great. I won the first challenge and got to go to an amazing restaurant tonight.

Alysse: Cool. I don't think you are supposed to tell me all this.

Staci: Oh. You're right. There's a guy here who—

Alysse: Cute?

Staci: Yes though that's not the problem. He really bothered me in the kitchen tonight. I'm worried. What if I screw this up?

Alysse: Maybe he got to you because you just didn't expect it. See what happens tomorrow, you know?

Good advice, Staci thought.

Staci: I'm so unsure and that's not like me.

Alysse: Stop it. You're the most powerful, kick-ass girl I know. You need to get him out of your head and you into his head.

Staci smiled to herself. It was a little late at night for Alysse's crazy outlook on life but she knew her friend's logic was sound.

Staci: Thanks. Heard from Jay?

Alysse: Not since yesterday but he said I wouldn't. I hate that he might be in danger.

Staci: He's coming back to you. And you both know it.

Alysse: Yeah. You okay now?

Staci: Yes. Thanks. Enjoy your brownies.

Alysse: I'm thinking of eating them all. :)

Staci: I suspected as much. Night.

Staci put her phone down and rolled over. The coolness of the air-conditioning circulated through the room making her feel as if she were on vacation. She and her grandmother didn't have air conditioning in their old fashioned ranch house. It had been built in the 50s and her grandmother had come to it as a young bride. The kitchen was the only thing that had been updated religiously by the women in her family.

Her grandpa had been killed in Vietnam, her father... well, she'd never known him.

The Rowland women had a weird legacy of being left behind by their men. She scrubbed her hand over her eyes and rolled over again.

"Hey, what are you the princess and the pea," Vivian grumbled from her bed.

"Sorry," Staci muttered. She'd never had to share a room with anyone. And she'd liked it that way.

The only way she'd have a room to herself was to out-cook everyone else. She forced her mind to cooking and the dishes she'd eaten tonight. Food had been her ticket out before and it would be again. WP24 was heavily Asian influenced and the tastes were familiar to her having grown up here on the West Coast. It was silly but she dreamed of food and cooking the way some women dreamed of shoes and purses.

What, she wondered, did Remy dream about? Was he like her and couldn't sleep when something new had been introduced to his palate? And why did it matter? She rolled over and heard Vivian sigh.

"Put your headphones in," Staci whispered. "I'm a very restless sleeper."

. The other woman grumbled as she took her iPhone headphones and put them in her ears. Staci grabbed her food diary as she thought of the night wind and the moonlight and the hot way that Remy had held her, touched her. She channeled that passion into food.

She heard the sea and tasted in her mind a new dish with seafood and spices but not from Mexico as she usually went to, but from China instead. There had been a wealth of new spices and tastes that had been brought to her tonight and now they were alive in her mind.

She wrote down ingredients, sketched in variations and maybes and then in her mind started to cook. She drifted to sleep with the pen in her hand and the notebook open on her lap. In her mind she was in the kitchen preparing her fresh ingredients. She smelled sesame oil heating up in a wok and glanced over to see Remy standing there waiting.

He'd chopped the garlic. "Let's cook together. I can help make this dish stronger."

She nodded and started telling him what to put in and he did exactly what she told him to do. They moved together in the kitchen, which, she noticed from the picture of her, her mom and her grandmother next to the stove, was her kitchen. He was talking and smiling in a way he hadn't when they'd cooked earlier and she started to resist the dream. This wasn't real.

She shoved him out of her kitchen and out of her mind waking up to find her flashlight and notebook on her lap. She didn't want or need Remy Stephens cooking with her. In real life or in her dreams, she needed instead to find her strength on her own. It was something she knew very well that she could do.

She closed the notebook and rolled over on her side to watch the shadows on the wall. She drifted in and out of sleep but it wasn't restful and in the morning when everyone started waking she was still tired.

She got dressed and hung out with the other women. Drinking coffee and talking about what they thought the challenge was going to be that day. She almost fooled herself into believing that she could handle Remy and that last night had meant nothing to her. However, when they piled into the cars to go to the studio, she ended up sitting right next to him and she knew she'd been lying to herself.

He smelled good. She hated that. She didn't want him to be one of those men who made her want to lean closer and breath more deeply.

"We have to talk about last night," he said quietly under his breath.

"Not now," she said. "We have to cook."

He nodded, but she knew he wasn't going to let it go for long.

"HELLO EVERYONE, I'M Fatima Langrene and I will be the host for the show. Each week we will start with a Quick Cook challenge," she said as they'd all been wired for sound and had their make-up done.

Fatima had mocha-colored skin and almond shaped eyes. He noted she also had a pretty smile and as she outlined the rules for this phase of the game, he knew he should pay better attention and did with one part of his mind.

But another part wanted to get some closure to what had happened with Staci. He needed to know that he hadn't hurt her. And that despite the timing, he wanted to see more of her.

"Our guest judge this week is Marcel Roubin, food critic from the *LA Times*. Mercedes is sponsoring this challenge so the winner will receive the keys to a brand-new M Class sedan. I'll let Marcel explain this challenge."

Marcel was skinny and wore all black clothing from the tips of his shining dress shoes to the color of his black dress shirt. His skin was pale in spite of the bright California sun.

"I knew it," Dan said under his breath, "He's a vampire."

Remy smiled.

"We all know you can cook with fresh ingredients and a well-stocked pantry but many in America are forced to create dishes for their family with only packaged and processed foods. Many families need new ideas to create something healthy and filling for their families from these ingredients," Marcel said, Taking the cover off a table that was laden with bags of frozen meats and vegetables.

"I mentioned Mercedes is sponsoring this Quick Cook challenge and they will be making a donation in the winner's name to the local food bank in your home town. You will have thirty minutes to create a main meal from these ingredients. Your time starts now."

Sizzle

Remy hadn't cooked with frozen ingredients ever but held hope there'd be some shrimp he could create a dish from. When he got to the table he saw that most of it was breaded or coated in seasoning already. He tried to think how to turn these mundane ingredients into a winning dish.

"My grandma used to make these fish sticks once a week," Staci said.

"Mine, too," Vivian added. "I don't know how I'm going to make them taste different but I'm starting there."

Staci smiled as she grabbed her choices and then, when she caught him staring at her, she winked. "Better get a move on, southern man. I'm planning to beat you today."

"Challenge accepted, cupcake girl," he said. He liked that they could still banter in the kitchen. That was how it should be. The personal stuff would have to wait for now. He grabbed some frozen shrimp and scallops, as well as a bag of frozen ravioli and went back to his station. The pantry was open but the shelves almost bare, except for dried herbs, butter, milk, and eggs. There were no fresh veggies so his idea for a Florentine pasta dish started to fade until he remembered there was frozen spinach. He grabbed what he needed and then ran back to pick up the spinach.

Ten minutes had already gone by and he hadn't even started removing the breading from the frozen seafood. He saw the other chefs around him similarly struggling, but a few of them were already cooking. Including Staci. He thought of her background, how she'd talked about

cooking with her grandmother and realized that the key
to this challenge was in something he'd never experienced before. He'd cooked from fresh and local ingredients because they were the best sources for good food.
Staci had done that because they'd been the quickest
and likely the cheapest.

He threw away everything he'd learned in the kitchen
and carefully considered the ingredients before him. He
needed to make something simple, healthy, yet tasty.
A Florentine dish was still his goal but he needed to
streamline it. He changed his main plan and discarded
the fish, opting for a single dish lasagna instead. He
heated up the prepared tomato sauce, which tasted too
bland so he went back to the pantry to get more spices
until the seasoning tasted as he wanted it. He layered
the heated sauce into the pan with the ravioli and the
spinach and then crumbled some cheese on top and put
it under the broiler to heat through and brown.

He pulled the dish out with two minutes left on the
clock. He sampled it and realized the dried spices and
processed cheese had yielded something that was very
tasty. He had never felt so free in the kitchen. This
wasn't something his grandfather, father or uncles had
ever done and as the timer sounded and he glanced at
the other stations he felt a certain confidence in both
himself and in his dish.

Marcel and Fatima started three stations down from
him and he glanced around the room, noting some interesting takes on the frozen food challenge. The sense
of pride he felt didn't wane. He knew his skills and the
dish he'd put together met the challenge requirements.

Marcel didn't like the dish that Max, who was at the station next to him, had prepared. "This shows little imagination. It's like you dumped the package on a cooking tray and prepared them per the instructions. I expected better from you."

"Everything is well cooked and I really liked the spices you added to the potatoes," Fatima said.

Now they were at Remy's station, staring at his dish. "What have you prepared?"

"A Florentine style lasagna, using prepared tomato sauce and ravioli."

Marcel didn't look like he was expecting much and Fatima just smiled at him. Remy realized that this was his first big cooking challenge all on his own. The world wouldn't end if he screwed this up, but then he'd never be more than the sum of his family. He'd never—

"Delicious," Fatima said. "What did you add to the sauce?"

"Spices and garlic," he said.

"It really is good," Marcel agreed. "I see you have seafood on your station why didn't you use it?"

"I was going to take the breading off and then I thought if I've worked all day and have hungry kids to feed, the last thing I'm going to want to do is take the bread off of some frozen shrimp. I want to feed the kids quickly and nutritiously. I would have wanted fresh spinach, but the frozen does still offer lots of nutrients," Remy said.

"Yes, it does." Marcel nodded.

The chef and host moved on to the next station and Remy caught Staci looking at him. He winked at her and she frowned at him. When the judges had tried all the dishes Remy, Staci and Conner had the top three meals.

"Our top three produced some really good and healthy dishes and all three will be presenting them at an LA Food Fair later this week. But today's winner is Staci."

Everyone clapped and Remy felt a pang of resentment that he hadn't won, but the smile on Staci's face made up for it. He wasn't happy to lose but he did like seeing her happy. Next time though he wanted her to have to be satisfied with second.

THEY TOOK A BREAK FROM filming after her win was announced. And the studio was cleared. Staci wanted to share her news with someone. Though as Alysse had reminded her last night, she wasn't supposed to share any details from the contest. All of the episodes were being taped to air once the entire competition was over.

"Another winning dish. Looks like you might be the chef to watch," Quinn said coming up to her. Quinn had been at the station next to her during the Quick Cook challenge and had made a faux risotto from boil in a bag rice. It had sounded pretty good but there hadn't been enough time to cook the rice and it had stuck together.

"I think each new challenge is going to up the stakes. So far they've been up my alley."

"Lucky," he said. "I wonder what the elimination challenge will be this week."

"From watching the show I thought they'd have told us already but I guess not," she said. She noticed Remy standing at the back of the room talking to Marcel. She'd heard—well everyone had—how much Marcel had enjoyed his dish and Staci was surprised that she'd beaten him.

"What's his story?" Quinn asked, gesturing toward Remy.

"Out of work New Orleans chef. I wonder if it's an effect of Katrina. I know that was years ago but I've heard from friends there that the city still hasn't recovered."

"Who knows? He's good," Quinn said.

Staci was getting a little annoyed at the way Quinn was talking about everyone else's skills and not his own. "Everyone's good or they wouldn't be here. You earned a spot just like everyone else. Shake off what just happened and focus on what you'll be doing next."

He gave her a half smile. "Sorry. I didn't sleep well last night. I don't like having to share a room."

"I don't either," Vivian said, joining their group. "The Princess and The Pea over here tossed and turned all night. But it didn't seem to affect your cooking."

"I don't need a lot of sleep," Staci said. "I've always been able to function on five hours."

Remy was lingering at the edge of the group. She tried to ignore him, wanted to show him he meant nothing more to her than any of the other chefs in the competition, but her heart beat a little faster and she found herself staring at him when she thought he wasn't looking.

"What's everyone's thoughts on the elimination challenge?" Remy asked.

"Well, I'm guessing an offsite test," Vivian said. "I

saw that they were bringing the cars around front for us. Plus they always start with that on the show."

"Do they?" Staci asked. "I've only watched a few episodes."

"Not me. I've been addicted to the show from the beginning. Love everything about it." Vivian smiled.

"Maybe we just have to go shop for our ingredients," Quinn suggested.

"I was hoping for a mystery basket," Staci said. She had done well with the first blind challenge after all.

"Doubt it after the Quick Cook," Vivian said.

"I don't care what it is as long as we start soon," Quinn said. "The waiting is hell."

The rest of the chefs continued talking and Remy took her arm and drew her away from the group. "Congratulations on your win."

"Thank you," she said. "I wasn't sure I could beat you. You had Marcel eating out of your hand."

"I was surprised. Critics don't usually go for easy comfort foods."

"No they don't but that was the spirit of the challenge," she said.

"Your mac and cheese looked good," he said.

"Thanks. Family recipe," she said with a quick grin.

"I gathered as much. Listen, Staci, I want to learn more about you. I like—"

"For the contest?" she asked.

He shook his head. "For me. I...I like you."

She backed away from him. "Not now. I said I don't want to talk about anything personal while we're here.

I need to stay focused on what I'm doing. Last night proved it to me. And I'm here to cook."

She wondered what he was hoping to find in her expression and then if he found it because he seemed to nod and take a step away. "All right, but when we get back to the house I want you to go for a walk on the beach with me."

She didn't want to commit to doing anything with him. She wanted to put distance between them but then remembered her dream last night. Remy was tied to her cooking now and she knew it. That passion he'd kindled in her last night was the fire that drove her whether she wanted to admit it or not.

"Fine. Let's get back to the others," she said.

They soon found out that Vivian was right. It was an Off-Site Challenge and they were headed to the UCLA college campus to serve lunch for the hungry students. They'd have to shop for their ingredients and then prepare them in two hours.

Staci tried to think of what she could make that would please the college students and the judges. But her mind was blank. She was thinking about Remy again and she had to wonder if that was his strategy. He'd certainly done a good job of distracting her. Ugh, she thought. She had to stay away from him. From now on when he walked over to her, she'd walk away.

They were driven to Whole Foods and everyone was shouting and running around like crazy people trying to find what they would need to create their dishes. Staci felt lost and she knew that after her win she was the one to watch so she took a second and pushed her trolley away from the crowds. She closed her eyes and thought about her grandmother, Alysse and all her friends back home in San Diego. She concentrated on them, but it wasn't calming her down.

"You okay, *chère*?" Remy asked coming up behind her with his buggy.

Suddenly she had an idea of what to cook and a new fire in her belly. She wasn't going to collapse in on herself. She was determined to win and to beat Remy again. She wanted him to see her, to know she was a good chef and she needed him to know that she was strong in the kitchen and out of it.

She gave him her sexiest grin. "I am now."

"Good. I'd hate to beat you if you aren't on your A game," he said.

"Ah, Southern Man, you're going to have a hard time beating me," she said. "That's a promise."

"Sounds more like a challenge," he said. "One I'm happy to accept. Whoever does better this afternoon— the loser has to cook dinner for them."

"Deal," she said. "I'm ready for you to have to cook for me."

"Pride goes before the fall," he said, pushing his trolley away.

And she just laughed as the dish finally coalesced in her mind. She didn't want to assign too much importance to Remy and instead decided that like a secret spice he was the key to her cooking. She realized that wanting to beat him and prove herself worthy in his eyes made the competition personal and that was what she needed.

6

SHE WON AGAIN AND AS SHE sat in the Escalade for the return trip to the Malibu house she was in a sort of stunned shock. While Staci knew she was capable of cooking, the win was confirmation that she had a real talent like her grandmother used to say. It was bittersweet though because she realized what she'd thrown away for "love".

"Congrats," Vivian offered. "I thought I had you at the last minute there when that pork you took off the grill was a little pink."

"Same here. I mean Austin barbecue is hard to beat. Everything was just flowing for me today," she said.

"I could tell. I tasted your dish and as much as it pains me to admit this, it was delicious."

"Thanks, Viv. Yours was good too," Staci said.

"I'm surprised Dave was in the top three," Vivian said. "Someone sure helped him with his butchering skills or he was sand-bagging last night...do you think he's clever enough to do that?"

Staci didn't know. She shrugged and pulled out her food journal to make a few notes about the dish she'd prepared. Because of the nature of the show she hadn't had time to make notes as she was cooking. With only an hour to cook there just wasn't time to analyze as she went along. One thing she had observed was that Remy had fallen back on another New Orleans taste that had cost him points in the final round according to the judges. She'd made an Italian flavored dish, which was very different from the food she'd been putting up before.

Beating Remy felt good of course because he challenged her and she wanted him to notice her and see her as the one to beat. But he'd looked angry and upset with himself after they'd announced she was the winner. That was something she didn't want for him.

Losing was hard. She'd certainly done it enough times when she and Alysse had been competing against each other in bake-offs. Staci would never have thought so at the time but that rivalry with Alysse had helped prepare her for this moment.

"I can't believe Quinn is in the bottom three. That was a shock," Vivian said. "Last night he put up a great dish."

"It's different cooking against the clock," Staci said still making notes in her journal. She didn't want to talk about the other chefs. Really the only one she was interested in had a slow southern drawl. She felt like maybe he hadn't been at his best today.

Had last night thrown him more than he wanted to admit?

She hoped so. She didn't want to think she was the only one who was making bad decisions and suffering for them. Yet at the same time she really hoped he wasn't affected by her. She wanted—no needed Remy to be a carefree kind of relationship. That would make it easier when they went their separate ways. To write off their encounter as just lust.

She turned to stare out the window and focused on the fact that all that training in Paris had been worth it. She'd have never guessed she could win a Mercedes by cooking, granted she'd achieved a lot in baking and even started her own business, but these were skills she'd avoided using since she'd left Chef Renard's kitchen all those years ago. Skills she'd associated with her poor decisions and resulting heartache. It was gratifying to know that sex with Remy didn't really feel like a mistake.

Even though she had absolutely no plans to do it again, she didn't regret it. Hell, she thought, glancing back down at her food journal, if sleeping with Remy raised her cooking to this level she might have to figure out how to sleep with him and not let her emotions get involved.

They got back to the house and all piled out of the Escalades. Staci tried not to watch for Remy but she couldn't help it. A part of her wondered if he still wanted to meet up with her this afternoon. But she knew he would. If she'd learned one thing about Remy in the short time since she'd met him it was that he never said anything he didn't mean.

"I guess you've got the judges where you want them," Quinn said. "Hard to believe a little cupcake baker is beating all of us."

"I'm—

"She's a skilled chef, Quinn. You can talk trash all you want but it's the dishes that we are all being judged on," Remy said in that quiet southern way of his. "She wouldn't have won if she hadn't deserved it."

"Whatever," he said, storming away from them.

Vivian lifted both eyebrows at her as if to ask *why's he defending you*? Staci just shrugged. She really didn't have a clue why he had, but there was a part of her that really liked what he'd done.

"Thanks," she said, as they climbed the steps into the house.

"Remy's right," Dave said.

"You did well today," Staci remarked to the other man.

"I just relaxed like Remy suggested. Stopped hearing the ticking of the clock in my head and I could think about the food," Dave said.

"Look at you, Remy, giving advice and defending chefs...."

Remy didn't say anything but entered the house and walked to the open-concept living room and specifically the bar. "I don't see the point in winning something if everyone's not playing up to par."

"I agree," Vivian said as she joined Remy pouring herself a gin and tonic. "What about you, Stac? What does our winner want to drink?"

"Diet Coke," she answered.

"And rum?" Vivian asked with a grin.

"No," she said. She still had to face a talk with Remy about last night and she would need all her wits about her. Everyone broke into groups as they discussed what they would make for dinner. It had a bit of a summer camp feel to it.

Because of her win everyone wanted to be around her and the afternoon passed in a blur as she chatted with all the chefs. Finally, most of the contestants went off to their own space while a few others left to walk on the beach or go surfing. Remy came over to her where she was sitting on a deck chair.

"Ready for that talk?" he asked.

No, she thought. At this moment she was at peace. The chaos in her mind was calm and she was enjoying the fact that she'd done the kind of cooking her grandmother would have been proud of her for doing. But she knew she had to deal with Remy and last night.

"I guess so."

"I'm not planning on torturing you," he said with a wry grin.

"I know. It's just at this moment...never mind. I'll sound silly if I say it." She got to her feet and started to lead the way down to the shoreline.

"There's nothing silly about you, Staci. I underestimated you, that's probably due to your size."

"Everyone always does. But as Shakespeare once said... Though she be but little she is fierce."

"He had it right. It's always funny to me how much of 17th century wisdom applies to life today."

"Do you know much Shakespeare?" she asked.

"I do. My mother is a high school English teacher and my father said that women like to hear a man read sonnets to them."

"And you believed him?" she asked.

"Well, he had at this point proven himself right about a few other things. I have never let him know that fact though. He has a big ego."

She laughed at the way he said it. She could tell from his words that he and his parents had a close relationship. She shouldn't be surprised, he had the persona of someone who had it all. A man who was very used to getting what he wanted. So what exactly did he want from her.

"Do you remember any sonnets?" she asked him as they reached the beach and started walking along the water's edge.

"Not any more," he said. "But I didn't want to quote Shakespeare for you. I wanted to discuss last night."

Of course he did. "What about it?"

"Do you want it to happen again?" he asked.

She stopped abruptly and turned to look up at him. "We aren't here for sex."

"No we're not, but there is something between us," he said.

She nodded. "I know you said that kissing me made you cook better in Chef Ramone's kitchen…"

"What are you trying to ask me? If I want to sleep with you again to cook better?" he asked, insulted that she'd think so little of him as a man. But then he realized that she didn't know the real him.

She bit her lower lip and then took an aggressive step toward him. "That's exactly what I want to know."

Remy saw bravado in her expression and knew despite the way she was playing it nonchalant that last night had meant more to her than a casual hook-up. The last thing he'd intended was to get involved with any woman during this competition. He was making a life-changing decision during his time in California and he needed to stay focused on that.

But he also knew that life had a way of nudging him in the direction he needed to go in and he wasn't sure exactly why he was so turned on by Staci Rowland, he only knew there was no denying it.

"I don't need sex to cook well," he said to her. "I've been cooking my entire life, but I've yet to find a woman who knocks me out of my comfort zone in the kitchen the way you did today."

"Really?" she asked, taking a step back and seeming to not notice the surf, which curled around her ankles and soaked the bottoms of her jeans. "I'm sorry."

"Don't be," he said, reaching for her hand and taking it in his, he started walking again afraid to say too much more. But he'd already revealed more than he should have given they were competitors. Yet lying about the attraction he felt for her wouldn't have sat well with him. "I just wanted you to know I'm not toying with you."

She took a deep breath. "I'm glad. I have to admit I was a little afraid that might be part of your strategy. Though to be honest it seemed to backfire on you today. What happened when you were cooking?"

"I don't know," he admitted. "I just fell back on my familiar tastes and dishes."

"And the judges didn't want that. I think they want us to grow…you know you owe me a dish. You have to cook for me."

"I know. What do you want me to make for you?" he asked.

"I don't know. Something that will make me forget everything I know about you. Make me a dish that will force me to see you in a different light," she said. "Like the tidbit about Shakespeare did."

"You liked that, didn't you?"

"Yes," she admitted. "You have a very nice voice I wouldn't mind hearing you recite a few sonnets for me."

"Maybe our next bet will involve that," he said.

She shook her head. "You don't want to hear me stumble over old English."

"Maybe I'll have you read something a little racier to me. I think there'd be nothing sexier than listening to you talk about your fantasies."

She flushed and shook her head. The wind stirred the short hair of her bangs. "I'm not…that is to say I don't—"

He laughed as he realized that the unflusterable Staci Rowland was uncomfortable talking about sex. She was flirty as hell and took what she wanted when they were intimate but there was a part of her that was shy when it came to the words.

"I can't believe you don't have fantasies," he said.

"Of course I do," she said. "Everyone does, but that doesn't mean I want to talk about them."

"I do."

"I'm not surprised. Despite what your father told you about sonnets you are still a man. Why is it men like to hear women talk like that?" she asked.

"It's sexy," he said. "And it's not every woman's fantasies I'm interested in."

She turned away again to glance out at the sea. He wondered, despite the fact that they were together here for six weeks, whether he'd ever really get to know all of her secrets. The core of Staci was very private. Would he be able to find out more about her through her cooking and her dishes? He doubted it. It felt to him like she was hiding herself away not only from him but from the world. She let him see what she thought he wanted to see.

The shyness with talking about sex was probably one of the first real things he'd been able to find out about her. She was all boldness and nerve but underneath there was a vulnerable woman.

He was being honest when he said that he wanted her and it had nothing to do with the competition but he saw now that that very fact made their relationship complicated. Did she even want to give him a chance?

"How do you feel about getting to know each other during the competition?" he asked. "I'm not trying to manipulate you."

She turned back to him her gray eyes as stormy as the Gulf of Mexico when a hurricane was blowing. "I don't know. I want to say no. I'm here to prove something to myself and to win. And I know it's the same for you."

"That's right. We both are cooking for our futures," he said. "I think everyone here is."

He noticed that she hadn't answered his question. Not really. He had the feeling that if he let her she'd never answer it. "I'm not going to ignore us, cupcake girl. I want you, but more than that I want to get to know you."

"I get it, but I'm not sure what to say. It doesn't matter if I say no and ask you to leave me alone. You're already under my skin. Dammit, I shouldn't have said that."

He laughed and tugged her off balance and into his arms, leaning down he kissed her with all the pent-up frustration he'd been feeling all day. When he lifted his head and stepped back her lips were swollen and her eyes half-closed. He wanted to carry her someplace private and make love to her. But he knew the next time he and Staci made love it would change things between them and there would be no going back.

"There's something between us," he said.

"I know. I wish it was just cooking," she admitted. "I have always had bad taste in men."

"Maybe your taste is changing," he said reluctant to let her lump him in with the other men who'd come before him.

I hope so, she thought. "I've been hurt in the past and I don't want to make the same mistake again, but then I always was a slow learner."

"What mistake?"

She shook her head. "That's not a story I'm willing to tell you."

"Just give me the Twitter version."

"A hundred and forty characters?" she asked, but she smiled at him.

"Yup."

"Thought that fairytales could come true and believed every word he said at hash tag shouldhaveknown-better."

"What kind of fairytale?" Remy asked.

"That there is one guy out there for me. One man who could make me complete and give me my happily-ever-after. But that's not realistic. I can't ignore the truth about the Rowland women.

"What truth is that?"

"We live alone," she said.

"What about your dad?"

"Never knew him or my granddad. None of the women in my family ever knew their fathers…do you know what that means, Remy?"

"I'm not that type of man."

"Are you making me promises?" she asked.

She wouldn't believe him if he did. Promises after all were just words and Staci needed, no, deserved action.

"No."

STACI WAS A LITTLE SURPRISED that he'd been so honest with her. A part of her had to respect his honesty. But the little girl inside of her who still wanted to believe in fairytales was disappointed that he hadn't stepped up. "I guess that's that."

"It is," he said. "I won't waste your time making you promises when you probably wouldn't believe them anyway. I'll just have to convince you that I'm not like the other men who've passed through your life."

She held her breath and her heart skipped a beat. Was he serious? Or was this just a ploy to make her believe…

he'd have to be cruel to say that type of thing…to get her hopes up only to plan to dash them later.

"Okay, prove it."

"I can't do it right now, can I?"

"No," she said. Thinking he probably never would. She wasn't going to pin any hopes on Remy. He was here for his own reasons, as was she. There was no point complicating things any further.

"We should be heading back."

"Not yet. I want you to show me around LA."

"Um, why?"

"We have the afternoon free and if I'm preparing a meal for you, I need to know more about you."

"Ha," she said. "How is walking around a city with me going to help?"

"I was thinking we'd go to the LA farmer's market."

"The good produce will already be gone. Besides it's more of a shopping center with permanent merchants."

"Then show me something that says LA to you," he said.

"I'm farther south," she said. "Los Angeles isn't really my town."

"I don't think the producers will let us drive to San Diego," he said with that half-grin of his that made her breath catch.

There was no denying he was a very attractive man. Even standing on the shore with the breeze ruffling his thick, black, curly hair just made him sexier. His eyes were shadowed by the sun. His T-shirt complemented his broad chest. His faded jeans hugged his legs and when he turned she let her gaze linger on his butt. She wanted to reach out and touch him but didn't. She had to keep control of herself. Until he proved to her that he wouldn't love her and leave her.

"Well?"

"Well, what?" she asked. Distracted by his body. She wished she'd gotten to see more of him last night.

"Where can we go that says LA to you?" he asked. "What are you thinking about?"

"Nothing," she said. Johnnie's in Culver City jumped to mind. It wasn't that far from where they were and the sandwiches were...well not really LA more New York Jewish Deli. The kind of thing that could transport the diner to another place. It was perfect to demonstrate what she'd said to him earlier.

"I've got an idea. I'll talk to Jack and see if we can get a car."

"Very well. I think we'll probably have to take others with us," he said. "I can't see the producers allowing just the two of us to go off on our own."

"I agree. That's okay, Remy. You'll figure out how to woo me even with others around."

"That's right," he said.

They walked back to the house and she was happy to finally be in the midst of the other competitors. There was a tension in the house probably because those in the bottom three would be cooking tomorrow to stay in the competition. She was glad that the only thing she had to think about tonight was Remy and not going home after the first week of competition.

She found Jack and asked him if they could make a trip to Johnnie's. Twenty minutes later he confirmed they could and seven of them headed to the Escalades. She was surprised that Quinn came with them. Thinking he'd want to stay behind and work on his knife skills like Christian and Frances who were also in the bottom three.

She was squeezed in the back seat between Remy and Quinn. She tried not to notice that she still loved the scent of Remy's aftershave. "Have either of you been to Johnnie's before?"

"Not me," Remy said. "This is my first time in Los Angeles."

"I've been here before but I tend to frequent the high-end restaurants," Quinn said. "I'm not surprised you like a walk-up diner."

"What's your problem with me?" she asked Quinn.

He shrugged. "I just don't see how someone with your tastes could beat me in the kitchen."

"My tastes? Quinn food isn't for the epicureans out there all the time. Today's challenge was to cook for college students. Do you really not get where you went wrong? It doesn't matter how obscure your ingredients are if the customer doesn't like it...that's cooking 101."

"She's got a point," Remy said. "I tried to introduce a new dish at my last restaurant and the clientele revolted. They wanted the dishes they'd come there expecting."

Quinn nodded. "I guess I wasn't seeing the big picture."

Staci smiled.

"I said I was wrong," he admitted.

"I don't want you to be wrong, just to stop blaming me because you didn't win."

He didn't say anything else on the drive and when they pulled up to the roadside diner on Sepulveda and everyone piled out of the vehicles, Remy took her hand and stopped her.

"What?"

"I just wanted us to be together when we go up there. What is it about this place that speaks to you?"

"The tradition of it," she said. "And it reminds me of a trip I took with my mom and grandmother to New York City. We ate in a diner there…it was a good trip. The only real vacation I had with my mom since she was working all the time. When I take a bite of the pastrami sandwich here I remember that day and her laughter."

Staci feared she'd said too much but Remy just nodded. "For me it's beignets at Café du Monde. My dad and I used to walk down there every Sunday morning and I'd sit while he read the paper. It was just the two of us…"

"Food should do that every time," Staci said. "I can't always capture it but that's why the traditional recipes are important. Finding that familiar flavor and taking it some place new."

"Yes," he said.

But Staci could tell that he was lost in his own thoughts. She wondered if she'd given away too much by bringing him here but then she had learned over the years that most people only saw what they wanted to in her and in themselves. Remy wouldn't realize how important food was to her and her past or that it was the key to all her secrets. He'd have to have been listening to what she hadn't said to figure that out. And he was after all just a man.

7

REMY KEPT HIS DISTANCE from Staci as they both returned to the house. He did some shopping in the pantry and started cooking. The contest seemed a little more real to everyone when faced with the fact that tomorrow one of them would be leaving.

That knowledge that any one of them could leave in a moment made Remy determined to make the most of his time with Staci. So he cooked for her remembering what she'd said about her mother and New York City. While he'd never been to Los Angeles before, New York and he went way back. One of his uncles owned an exclusive cooking school there and Remy had spent three weeks every summer in the meatpacking district honing his chef skills.

There were others with him working in the kitchen now but none of the jovial talking of the night before. The competition had gotten serious today. Christian, one of the chefs in the bottom three, was tirelessly going over the same sauce he'd made earlier in the day. The sauce that had netted him horrible reviews.

Christian had a carefully trimmed beard and dark brown eyes that seemed to view the world wearily. He was tall but not as tall as Remy's six-foot-three frame and a little bit stocky. He moved almost awkwardly when he wasn't at his station. But once he had a knife in his hands his skills came to the fore.

"Have you figured it out yet?" Remy asked, when he noticed the chef had stopped scribbling in his notebook.

"Just about. I have no idea what they are going to throw at me tomorrow but sauces have long been my weak point. I can muster a buerre blanc but that's about it. I should have known better than to try one today."

"You did what you had to in order to win."

"Did I?"

"Yes, you have to push yourself. That's what I realized today. I can't just do what I've always done," Remy said. It was nothing less than the truth and he wished he'd figured that out earlier. More than likely that was part of the reason for his reluctance to take over as Chef Patron of Gastrophile. He had tried to introduce new dishes but today he'd realized he'd done that in the wrong way. There was a way to put his stamp on the restaurant without eviscerating what had gone before. And that was the key.

"True enough. I'm in the same boat. Cooking was always easy for me when nothing else was. This is the first time I've flat-out failed. I don't like it."

Remy laughed. "I don't either. I'm too used to winning."

Christian smiled over at him. "I'd take third over bottom three."

"I bet you would. Next time we'll both be in the top three."

"Next time, I'll be number one," Christian said. "I'll leave you to your cooking."

Remy finished his dish and then put everything in plastic containers and packed it in a cooler he found in the pantry. He left it sitting on the counter and went to find Staci. She was sitting on the edge of her bed with her notebook open reading over her notes. He stood there for a long minute just staring at her. Though it had only been a few days his impression of her had changed radically from that first moment they'd met and she'd spilled tea all over the both of them.

Yet one thing hadn't changed. He still wanted her and would continue to want her he suspected no matter how many times he had her. There was something almost elusive about the woman. Something that he just couldn't shake no matter how many times he tried.

He noticed the way her jet black hair was tucked behind her small ear and the long curve of her neck. The t-shirt she wore hugged her breasts and then her tiny waist. Her legs were curled under her in a position that he doubted he'd be able to make if he tried for hours.

"Like what you see?" she asked, a hint of humor in her voice.

"You know I do, *chère*," he said, taking his time and letting his gaze slide back up her body. She shifted on the bed, uncurling those shapely legs and standing up.

"Your dinner is ready," he said, bowing slightly.

"Great. I'm interested to see what our field trip this afternoon has inspired in you."

It wasn't the food that was inspiring him and he knew that now. If he'd had this new knowledge and his wits about him during the UCLA challenge he wagered he'd have won today. But he hadn't. He could only use it to make sure he kept himself in the top three and moving forward with each week of competition.

"I hope you will be surprised," he said.

"I'm sure I will be. It's rare that I've had a man cook for me," she said, following him down the hall to the kitchen.

Given the little he knew of her personal history that wasn't a real surprise. "The men you've known haven't been chefs."

"One of them was," she said almost beneath her breath.

He lifted the cooler and led the way through the open living room to the back patio. "We can eat here…or down on the beach where we will have more privacy."

"I vote for the beach," she said. "I don't want everyone to know that we are dining together."

"Why not?"

"People will talk," she said. "It doesn't matter that there are no rules against fraternizing, I know how unkind gossip can be. I think we'd both fare better if we keep this private."

He nodded. He thought so, too. Besides he didn't want to share Staci with anyone else. There was something intense about his attraction to her. He wanted to know more about her and it occurred to him as they walked down the beach to find the perfect spot for their picnic away from the other beach goers that he had created a dinner tonight to seduce her. He should have guessed.

Food was one of the most sensual experiences for him. He spread out the blanket he'd taken from the linen closet and watched as Staci sat down in the center of it. He set the cooler next to her before sitting down.

He opened the cooler to take out the bottle of wine that he'd wrapped in a chilled towel and had positioned on the cool side of the cooler. He deftly opened it and then took out the two stemmed glasses and poured them each a glass.

Staci took one from him. "I'll say this for you, you picked the perfect place for dinner. Light breeze, setting sun…I'm almost seduced just sitting here."

"Almost is the key word, by the time this meal is over you will be totally seduced."

"I'm not too sure about that, but I like your confidence."

"I like yours as well," he said. If there was one quality that always shone through in Staci it was her belief in herself. He admired her for it. He knew she'd worked hard for that, unlike himself, who'd had it assumed of him that he'd be good just because of his DNA.

"A toast to confidence and ego and hoping there's room enough in the kitchen for both of ours."

He smiled and lifted his glass toward hers. "To confidence."

He noticed that she kept eye contact when she took her first sip of the wine. It was something that his father said only people with great gumption did. The wine was dry and cold just the way he liked it.

"Ready to be impressed."

"Always," she said.

He pulled out the dishes he'd packed and the containers. "While I'm getting our dinner ready why don't you tell me something about the other chef you mentioned."

Her hand shook as she was taking a sip of her wine and a drop of it spilled onto her lip. She stared over at him and he wondered what he'd said that upset her. "I assume it was just another man who didn't cherish you."

THE LAST THING THAT STACI wanted to talk about was the past but today Jean-Luc Renard seemed to be everywhere. But she knew she had to at least say something. Remy had gone to more effort with this meal side-bet they'd had than she'd expected.

Her hand trembled again. Was she seriously thinking they might be a couple? She thought of how she handled her relationship with Alysse and they had a business contract as a safety net to ensure that Alysse lived up to her side of the bargain. Though now that she knew Alysse she understood the other woman would never leave her hanging.

But she hadn't known that at first. And weary of being hurt again she'd done everything she could to protect herself. She'd come away from Sweet Dreams Bakery with the belief that she could trust women but not men. Now she was looking at Remy and wondering if she could trust him.

She wanted to.

"Are you going to take the plate or simply keep staring at it?" he asked, his voice quiet as if he sensed she was dwelling on deep thoughts.

She wanted to scream at frustration with herself. Any other woman would just enjoy the night and the romance of it but she was weighing his every move against her tender heart and trying carefully to get to know him while protecting herself. It was harder than it should be because she felt as if she could believe him.

She wanted Remy Stephens to be just what he appeared to be—an out-of-work chef who could cook like nobody's business and charm her socks off.

"Yes, I'm going to take it. The food smells delicious," she said.

"I hoped you'd like it. Why don't you save your story of past loves for another night?" he suggested. "I don't want you thinking about another man while savoring my dishes."

She nodded. She didn't want to think about Jean-Luc either. And one thing that made it easier to ignore her past lover was the fact that three-star Michelin chef that he was, he'd never cooked for her. That should have been her first clue that what they had wasn't real...

"What have you prepared?"

"New York City," he answered with that rogue's grin of his. "You said your happiest memories were associated with your mother and that city."

"You know New York?" she asked. "How does someone from New Orleans become familiar with a big city like that?"

"I do get out of the bayou occasionally," he said wryly.

"I didn't mean it like that. Sorry, it's just you seem very rooted in the South," she explained. "It's a surprise that's all."

"Well taste it and tell me if it's a good surprise or not," he said.

She shook off the mantle of the past and instead concentrated on the now. Remy hadn't proven himself to be anything other than a white-hot lover, first-class chef and a really nice guy who liked her. She set her wine glass down on the tabletop Remy had made with the cooler lid and took the heavy silver fork he'd passed to her.

Carefully she arranged a bite of the meat, which was breaded and had a sauce on it, the creamy risotto and lifted it to her mouth. It smelled incredible and her mouth was already watering. When she opened her lips she noticed that Remy stared at her mouth. She let her tongue dart out to taste the food before taking the first bite.

His eyes narrowed and suddenly she was lost in the food as the feeling of New York City was on her palate. The food had that warm comfort that Staci had always gotten from her mother, but also the edge that she'd felt when in New York. She closed her eyes and forgot about everything and admitted that if he cooked like this next week then she and the other contestants were out of the running.

"It's good," she said at last, well aware that her words were faint-praise for the dish she'd just sampled.

He nodded. "Thanks. I won't let all the effusive praise go to my head."

"Like you need me to tell you that you're good," she said. "The dish is New York, but my experience there. How did you do that?"

He leaned over and touched the side of her face. As if she could ever not pay attention to Remy Stephens.

"I listened to you," he said. "Everything that you said this afternoon about food memory made me realize I was missing a powerful spice in my chef's kit. And it was the personal experience."

"Memo to self—stop giving Remy advice if you want to win this competition," she said with a rue grin.

He laughed as she'd hoped he would but it didn't lessen the tension inside of her. Somehow she knew it was the mere mention of her lover in Paris that cast a damper over her spirits. She'd thought that almost six years would be long enough to dull not only his memory but his hold over her but she was realizing it wasn't.

She guessed there were some wounds that cut too deep. But she also knew that there were so many elements in this very situation with Remy that were similar to how she'd fallen for Jean-Luc. The food, the passion for cooking…that very Gallic outlook on life that they both shared.

"I think you'll do just fine. You have some of the best cooking instincts I've ever seen. My grandfather would have loved to have you apprentice in his kitchen."

"Who is your grandfather?"

Remy bit his lip and looked away from her and down at his plate for a minute. "No one really, just an old chef who said to me that cooking comes from the soul but until I heard you talk about it I never got what he meant."

"So you're saying I remind you of your grandpa?" she asked.

"Not in the slightest. But you do have the same gut instincts he does. I think he'd be very impressed by you," Remy said.

"Are you impressed?" she asked. She wanted to groan after she said it but she also really wanted him to like her. To see all of her talents and none of her flaws. Dammit, she thought. She was already starting to hope that he could be the man she saw tonight. A man who had the same goals, the same soul as she did. It was something that she really needed to work on if she was going to have any chance of protecting herself from falling for Remy.

"*Chère*, you've done nothing but wow me since the moment you fell into my arms," he said.

They both finished up their dinner and then Remy stowed the dishes back into the cooler. She noticed that he kept everything as neat and tidy as he did his mis en place when they were cooking. "You are very neat."

"That's a good thing in a chef," he said.

"Yes, but even away from the kitchen. Why is that?" she asked. It might be nothing but then again it could be the key to figuring out Remy.

"My father said a man who lacks the discipline to keep himself tidy lacks the discipline to run a kitchen."

"And that was your goal?" she asked.

"It was my heritage," he said.

There was gravitas in his voice and she wondered what kind of expectations his family must have put on him. The disappointment they'd feel that he was out of work now. He needed this win, she thought, almost as much as she did.

"From your Creole family?"

"Most definitely," he replied.

She took his hand in hers. "You're a great chef, Remy. No one can take that from you and no matter if you are the head chef in New Orleans most famous restaurant or the purveyor of street food in New York you're still honoring your talent."

REMY WAS FLATTERED BY what she said and it was a sentiment his grandmother would have echoed but his father, his grandfather and his uncles they had a different plan for Remy and his future. They wanted him to take up the mantle of Chef Patron and continue the tradition of the kitchen that had won three Michelin stars. And for the first time, Remy understood that he might not want that path.

He'd come here with seemingly one goal, one objective, yet from the second he'd met Staci all of that had changed. It didn't matter what he'd told himself in the past, there was something in this moment that felt like truth. It felt like his life was changing and he hadn't experienced that outside of the kitchen before.

He moved around on the blanket until he was positioned behind Staci and drew her into his arms so that her back was pressed to his chest. She sat stiffly at first. So all the seducing he'd done with his food hadn't made her relax with him. Sex, he thought, might have created more barriers between them than he'd thought.

For all her tough-girl attitude there was a soft inner

core to Staci that she protected like a fierce warrior. His intuition told him it was because she'd been hurt before…disappointed by people in general. But more than that. He remembered what she'd said about no man in her life having stayed. No father or grandfather. No boyfriend.

And though he knew his intentions were honorable there was a part of him that knew he had to be very careful. He had no idea if this attraction was just the excitement of being in a new place and meeting a type of woman he'd never encountered before. He was old enough at thirty to know himself and what he wanted but he had no idea if he could tame Staci and convince her he was a staying kind of man.

Or if he wanted to. The fact was he was lying to her by not telling her his real name and background. And a part of him knew he should say something to let her know but he couldn't risk anyone else knowing who he was. And the secret was his burden. If at some point his true heritage in cooking became known he didn't want her to have to pay the price for not coming forward sooner.

His reasons all sounded good to him but another part of him knew that as long as he kept his secret this life, this idyllic time with Staci could continue. He didn't have to try to figure out the logistics of falling for a woman who lived on the West coast. He didn't have to face the fact that his life was always going to be in New Orleans and she was as deeply entrenched here. He kind of enjoyed the freedom of being Remy Stephens instead of Remy Cruzel. Remy Stephens could stay.

"Do you see that constellation?" he asked.

"Yes. Orion, right?"

"Yes, the hunter. It's the most visible of all the constellations, you can see it anywhere in the world. When I was young, my father had to travel for a few years and every night he'd tell me to look up at this constellation and know that he was doing the same. That we were together even though we were miles apart."

She relaxed against him as he told her more about the night sky. He didn't know much but he'd already figured out that with Staci sharing parts of himself was the key to getting past her barriers.

"My mother and I did that with the moon. She'd send me a kiss to the moon and I'd retrieve it when I went to bed…" she said, her voice wobbled a little. "I've never told anyone that before."

"It's okay. Your secret is safe with me," he said.

She shifted around to look at him. "I want to believe that but the past has taught me that a secret is only safe if you keep it."

He had just thought the very same thing and he knew that a man who was busy trying to cover up something had no ground to stand on. He leaned down to kiss her because it seemed a better thing to do than to make promises he knew he couldn't keep. He wanted to tell her he'd never lie to her but since he already was…

Angry at himself for not being able to be the man he wanted to be with her, he slipped his tongue deep into her mouth. Trying to show her the truth the only way he could at this moment. He wanted her but more than that he liked her, he respected her, he was in awe of her.

He wanted her to be the woman in his life despite the fact that they were both competitors and going after the same prize.

While he wasn't ready to throw in the towel and concede victory to her he knew that if she won, he wouldn't be as disappointed as he might have been a mere week ago. He'd already learned more about himself in the last few days then he had in the last four years of doing the same thing every day.

He put his hands on her waist and hugged her close to him as he lifted his head. Her lips were swollen and her eyes closed. "That nearly got out of hand."

"Did it? I thought that might have been your plan for the evening," she said.

"No. I want to get to know the real Staci Rowland so the next time, when I take you to my bed…and it will be my bed and I can have the time to explore your body, we both understand it's more than just attraction."

She turned in his arms and put her hands on his shoulders leaning down close to him. "You keep saying the right things…"

"Is that a problem?" he asked, keeping his hands on her waist even though he wanted to slide them around to her ass and draw her in closer to him. He wanted to feel her straddling him and claim another kiss to stir the passion that was between them.

"No. But I've heard it all before. The lies, the lines. And a part of me wants to believe you are different, Remy, but you're a guy."

"Yes, *chère*, I am. And one you've never known before."

She shook her head. "You've got a point but in my experience every man is hiding something and my gut says you're the same."

He swallowed hard and knew that if he told this lie it would hurt him later but he decided he could make up for it. Staci needed him to be a man she could believe in. She needed a man to prove to her that there was more to a relationship than sizzle and he was determined to be that man.

She turned back around and he held her in his arms but this time as she settled back against him he didn't feel the peace of the night or the need to share past memories. Instead his mind was active with the thought that sooner or later he was going to have to tell her who he really was. But when?

8

THE HOUSE WAS A BEEHIVE of activity when they returned from their walk on the beach. Though things had gotten hot and heavy they hadn't made love and Staci felt unnerved by that. She was also feeling what she knew was the first flush of love. She couldn't help smiling every time she looked over at Remy as they sat in the living room with the other chefs.

Some of the contestants were already clearly working on a strategy by talking about their own skills and pointing out the weaknesses of others. It wasn't as if she didn't expect it from them. After all they were being taped all the time they were in the house and it was a television show so some tension was a good thing. But she wasn't interested in that side of the game.

She was more focused on winning by cooking and if she were being completely honest Remy.

"Next week will be interesting. Staci, you're the one to watch. What do you think the next challenge will be?" Viv asked.

"Not sure. I've been as surprised as you guys so far," she said.

Staci preferred to do all of her talking in the kitchen rather than speculating on what might be coming up. Whatever it was, the challenge would be to keep her cooking fresh. She glanced over at Remy. After eating the dinner he'd prepared tonight she knew he was probably her toughest competition.

"They change it up every season. I really want a mystery basket," Dave said.

Conversation flowed around her as everyone discussed his or her favorite type of cooking. Christian, Quinn and Frances were all quiet no doubt dwelling on the fact that the next day they'd be cooking to stay in the competition.

Slowly, everyone got up to go to bed and she left after Remy did. There were too many people around for a private goodnight and Staci was okay with that. Since they were in the house now they weren't a couple. Were they anywhere else?

But she knew that they were. At least in her eyes. She wondered if her mother had felt this way with her father. Staci had always wondered why her mom hadn't seen the signs that her father wasn't going to stay. But the feelings swamping Staci now made her realize that love came whether it was wise to get involved or not.

Staci could only hope that she had chosen better than both her mother and grandmother. She was still feeling not exactly happy with her new feelings for Remy when Vivian walked in.

"I noticed you and Remy were getting cozy tonight,"

Vivian said after she'd washed up and they were both sitting on their beds.

"Yes. I…he and I had a bet and he had to cook me dinner since I won the challenge."

"Did you learn anything you can use from his cooking?" Vivian asked.

"I did. But that's not why I did it."

"It should be. Unless you're not here to win. And given the way you are cooking I'm pretty sure that's the only reason you are here."

"You're right, but I think…"

Vivian shrugged. "I'm the last one to give another woman advice on a man but you should watch your back. Everyone here is playing an angle."

"Even you?" Staci asked.

"Hell, yes."

Was Remy still playing an angle? It would be easier for her to believe in that than to trust him. But it almost felt like it was too late to stop the feelings that were welling up inside of her. She didn't want to be a fool again.

She needed to keep her distance. Starting tomorrow she'd back away. It was the only smart thing to do.

"What's *your* angle?"

"Don't give away my strengths," Vivian said. "Not even to you, girlie!"

Staci smiled at her. "Come on, Viv. You can trust me."

"Is that what Mr. Man said to you?" she asked. "I'm not trusting anyone. I like you but when it comes down to it, there can only be one winner and I'm going to be champion."

Staci realized that what Vivian said was true. But there was more to life than winning. In five weeks the prize would be handed out and either way, win or lose, she was getting on with her new life. She'd already started pulling out of the day-to-day running of Sweet Dreams so she could pursue new directions. This show…her time here was supposed to help her decide where to go next. Would that be enough though?

Her new feelings for Remy could influence where she ended up but truly was she going to follow a man she'd met on a cooking show? She knew she had to figure out her priorities. She'd already decided to put some extra distance between them and as of this instant she understood that it wasn't just a good strategy for the game but also for her life.

The only person she'd ever truly trusted had been her grandma and when Rosalyn had died Staci had been alone in the world. Her mother, albeit kind hearted, had never been emotionally stable enough for Staci to lean on and she had to remind herself that the only one she could count on was herself.

That didn't mean she regretted anything with Remy. It simply meant that she was going to remember the truth behind every emotion. He was doing what was right for him. She had to do what was right for herself.

"Well, I hate to break it you, Viv, but I'm going to do my level best to beat you and if today is any indication I think I'm off to a good start."

"You are, girlie, but the judges now expect a higher standard from you. You'll have to keep cooking up to it."

Staci wasn't worried, even brokenhearted and alone

she'd always been able to keep a clear head in the kitchen. This would be no different.

"We will see next week, won't we?"

"Yes, we will," Vivian said. She got under her covers and curled up on her side. "I hope I didn't speak out of turn saying what I did about Remy. It's just I don't want to see a chef as good as you go home because of a man."

She got under her covers too and reached over to turn out the lamp on her nightstand. She'd already thrown away one chance because of a man, she didn't want to let it happen again.

"Me, either," she said rolling over and punching her pillow but it didn't relieve the frustration flowing through her. She'd started to believe that Remy was different but listening to Vivian was like talking to herself. She knew that men lied. It made sense that he'd be playing an angle. They were competitors after all. But the man who'd held her tenderly and told her about his father and the constellation…that man she wanted to trust.

Promising herself she was smart enough not to make the same mistake twice. Promising herself that she'd be cautious where Remy was concerned. Promising herself that she'd weigh everything he said to her and not just trust him blindly.

Vivian slept restlessly and her dreams were tortured visions of the kitchen in Paris. Remy and Jean-Luc were both there watching her cook and then tasting her dishes and judging them to not be good enough.

And a part of her woke to the feeling that she was determined to prove that this time she was going to be the one who judged them. This time she'd walk away the winner. This time she wasn't going to risk her heart so easily.

REMY HAD SUSPECTED THAT things wouldn't be as easy as they'd seemed that night on the beach, but he hadn't anticipated Staci ignoring him or how he'd react to it. Frances had gone home and the next week of competition had pitted the men against the women in a restaurant challenge. Each team had to choose a captain, plan a menu and then run a pop-up restaurant for one night. The diners ate in both restaurants and voted on their favorite dishes. Whichever team had the most votes would win the team challenge and whichever chef produced the favorite dish would win the individual prize.

The men had chosen Christian fresh off his win in the bottom three challenge to be the leader. The women had chosen Staci. Remy wasn't surprised but he did wonder how the mantle of leader would sit with her.

He tried to steal some time alone with her but she was careful to keep her distance from him. Perhaps he should be doing the same thing instead of trying to catch her attention. He focused on his dish. Remembering everything he'd learned in the previous week and in a lifetime of cooking. He created a dish to please his palate. Not being in charge of the team meant he could stand back and just cook. Which turned out to be a good thing because there was a lot of testosterone in the kitchen. He stayed clear of Conner and Quinn, who were in a battle to prove each was a bigger egomaniac than the other.

Christian did his best to lead but it was clear to Remy

that the other man's strength was really in the creation of the menu and the front of the house. He charmed every patron who entered their restaurant and it wasn't long before Remy believed that they would win.

Until he heard the laughter and compliments coming from the women's side. Just that was enough for Conner and Quinn to put their egos aside and start working together. No one wanted to lose this challenge.

"The judges are here," Christian shouted, coming into the kitchen. "I've just seated them. Chefs, we need your very best!"

They all cooked and plated their food and there was no time to wait for feedback from the judges as other customers were waiting to be served, but they sent back the appetizer that Conner had prepared. Which didn't sit well with the other man. It worried Remy since he knew the dish had been well prepared until he learned there was a shell in the seafood pate that Conner had created.

An error, Remy thought. That was something that Conner should have caught before the dish was sent to the floor.

But the other man had been too focused on other things…just as he Remy had been with Staci in the Quick Cook. The only way to win this, and that was still his objective, was to do as Staci was doing and put her from his mind.

But that was harder than he'd anticipated. His dreams had been filled with steamy visions of Staci in his arms on the beach. He'd been tormented by the memory of her soft warm body wrapped around his.

"You're up, Remy. Three mains."

He started cooking, remembering making love to Staci and when he plated his dish he knew he'd created something that had its roots in what they had both experienced together. He sent the dishes out with the waiter and tried not to stand there like a first time chef.

None of the dishes came back and the rest of the night passed in a blur. Soon they were back in the *Premier Chef* kitchen. There was a tension in the stew room as they waited to be called in front of the judges. Staci jotted notes frantically in her journal. Others drank water like it was cheap vodka. Finally Fatima entered the room.

"We're going to do individual judging first and then teams. We'd like to see Vivian, Remy and Gail."

Remy got to his feet more nervous than he wanted to be. He knew he'd cooked a great dish but he hadn't exactly hit a home run with the judges thus far.

"Now it's time to see if we're the winners or the losers," Vivian said. "But if we're the bottom three then there is something wrong with them. I know I didn't screw up today."

"We will just have to see," Remy said.

"Yes, we will."

They entered the judging room where a long table sat with the three judges behind it. Fatima took her spot next to them and Jack, the director gave them all marks to stand on. In this moment he really resented the fact that this was a TV show. He wanted them to just deliver the news—good or bad. But they had to be set up and then wait.

Eventually, the production crew were in their spots

and Fatima smiled at them. "Congratulations, the three of you had the top dishes."

"I know that," Vivian muttered.

Relief coursed through Remy. He was very happy to know that he'd made a good showing today. A part of him, just a tiny part felt bad that Staci wasn't in here. But perhaps being the leader of her team had distracted her from cooking.

The judges all took turns telling them why they liked their dishes before Fatima announced that Remy had won the challenge.

"From the first dish you put up, we knew you could cook," Hamilton said. "But tonight you showed us something fresh and new. Good job."

"Thank you, chef."

"You're welcome," Hamilton said.

"We need you to send back a few of your colleagues."

"Certainly," Remy said.

They asked to see Tony, Ashley and Conner. Remy had a feeling that Conner might be going home. Although he had no idea how bad Ashley's dish was. Tony's dessert hadn't set right but Remy had tried it and presentation aside it had tasted really good. He was thrilled they didn't ask to see Staci. He wanted her to stay in the competition. He wondered if their date had been a distraction for her. And decided he'd keep his distance as she clearly wanted him to.

They returned to the stew room and sent the three chefs to see the judges after Remy announced he'd won.

"I heard them raving about your dish," Staci said when he sat down.

"The judges?" he asked.

"No. The diners. There wasn't one who didn't talk about the main and how delicious it was. I thought that must be Remy's dish. Did you make them what you made for me?"

"No," he said. "That was just for you, *ma chère*. But I did use the advice you gave me. By talking about food and memories you reminded me that there is more to cooking than technique."

Staci smiled. "Given that you won, maybe I should have kept my mouth shut."

"Maybe you should have."

"I'm glad I didn't," she said.

"Why is that?" he asked.

"Now that you've upped your game everyone has and the competition feels more unpredictable. These challenges really shake us up and force us to focus on the food. That gets lost in the day-to-day working of the kitchen, you know?"

"I do indeed," he said.

The three chefs re-entered the kitchen and they were told that Conner had the least favorite dish and was going home.

"They want to see the rest of you," Conner said. "The cook-off will be between the bottom three on the losing team. Good luck, guys."

Everyone said goodbye to Conner and then they all went back to the judges room. The comments started out harsh but then ended on an upbeat note. The contestants were given a chance to defend themselves but everyone owned up to their mistakes. The women lost the round and Staci, Kristi and Whit were the bottom three.

STACI WON HER QUICK COOK with Kristi going home, but the next week was back in the bottom three again. A part of her wanted to blame Remy but he'd kept away from her which was all she'd wanted. They had a free day and Staci knew she should be in the kitchen practicing but she had the feeling her head was getting in her way. It was as if she'd forgotten all the things she really knew about cooking.

Remy walked up to her where she sat in the living room watching Sponge Bob with Dave.

"Pack your bathing suit and meet me out back in ten minutes."

"Um…why?"

"Because it's our day off and we need to talk and to get out of this house."

Remy had won the last two weeks and he was clearly hitting his stride at the right time. "You don't owe me anything."

"Go get changed. The clock is ticking," he said.

She wasn't sure that going out with him was a wise idea but ignoring him hadn't exactly been working for her either. She pushed to her feet and went to change. Putting on her black bikini and covering it up with a pair of denim shorts. She grabbed her sunglasses and put on a pair of Roxy flipflops before heading out back to meet Remy.

He'd swapped clothes for a pair of blue board shorts and left his shirt off. Oh, the man was ripped. His chest muscles drew her attention and she didn't want to look away. It was the first time she'd seen his chest. She'd touched him, true enough, but now she knew what he looked like. She understood why he'd said the next time they made love it would be in a bed. She wanted the chance to explore his body, too.

He glanced over at her as she approached, his gaze skimming over her body. "Ready?"

"Yes," she said. "What are we doing?"

"You'll see. I arranged for us to go sailing."

"I'm not really that proficient on a boat."

"That's okay. I hired a crew."

"Can you afford that?" she asked.

"Let me worry about that," he said. When they got to the beach he directed her toward the pier where there were a number of yachts tied up. Suddenly she was feeling a bit underdressed in her bikini top and denim shorts but Remy took her hand in his and led the way to a large yacht.

He helped her onboard and directed her to a padded bench in the back of the boat. "I'll be right with you."

"Um…where are we going?" she asked.

"Away from the world," he replied disappearing below deck. She took a seat where he'd directed her and tried to relax. It was harder than she'd expected because she felt unsure of what Remy was up to.

He'd been keeping to himself for weeks, now they were on a luxury yacht. She took out her cell phone and texted Alysse.

Staci: You'll never guess where I am.

Alysse: Where?

Staci: On a yacht…with Remy. Is this a mistake? Tell me to jump overboard and swim for shore.

Alysse: Ha. Stay there and enjoy your time with him. The competition is just heating up and he must like you if he's wooing you."

Staci: I'm scared.

Alysse: Men are like that. Remember how afraid I was to trust Jay.

Yeah, but Jay loved Alysse. Jay had come back to town to win her friend's heart and make a new life with her. This was totally different. She heard footsteps and glanced up to see Remy approaching with a champagne glass in each hand.

Staci: TTYL

Alysse: Like I said, relax and enjoy it.

Staci doubted that was going to happen. She'd let Vivian's words and her own natural reticence take over and she knew that it was going to be hard to be calm around Remy. She didn't know if he was sincere even though he did seem to be. But then she'd never had a good radar to judge when a man was lying.

She put her cell phone back in her bag as Remy sat down next to her and handed her the champagne. "I realize we should be dressed more formally but I didn't want to give my surprise away."

"And what exactly is your surprise?" she asked as the boat's engines were fired up.

"A day out at sea, just the two of us. I took the liberty of securing permission with Jack for us both to be gone until ten tonight."

"All day at sea?" she asked.

"I thought we could go swimming and sunbathe. And just have a chance to get to know each other away from the house. A chance to take a break without thinking about the competition," he said.

"You know the water in the Pacific is cold unlike the Gulf of Mexico," she warned him.

"I do. I have wet suits for us both. Have you ever tried spear fishing?" he asked.

"No. Have you?"

"Yes. In the Bahamas with my grandfather. I'd like to show you," he said.

In for a penny, in for a pound. "Why not? Given the way I've been cooking I could go home next week and then I wouldn't see you again, would I?"

"At least not until the competition is over. I can't think beyond that but I do know that I want to enjoy every moment with you," he said. "And I think you want the same. That's why ignoring each other isn't working for us. We need to pay attention to this part of ourselves. You are constantly on my mind and my body aches for yours, *ma chère*."

"You seem to have done a good job of ignoring your desires and cooking up a storm," she said.

"That's an illusion," he said. "I've missed you."

She didn't know what to say to that. A part of her had missed him too but she really had her hands full. All of her energy either went to cooking or ignoring him. Maybe he had a point about why that wasn't working.

He handed her the champagne flute and lifted it to her. "To new beginnings."

"New beginnings," she said, taking a sip of the

champagne as they sailed farther away from the shore. "Where exactly are we going?"

"Trust me," he said. "The captain said we have a thirty minute ride to where we will try fishing. Why don't we sunbathe?"

"Okay but this is nice."

"It is but I want to see all of you," he said.

"All of me?" she asked, realizing he was talking about her denim shorts. "And maybe help me put on some sunscreen?"

He laughed. "I'm obvious, aren't I?"

"A little."

"It's true I relish the thought of running my hands over your curvy body. You need to relax. I've never seen anyone more tense than you are with each passing day."

"I'm struggling to find some balance. And it's hard to always be on your guard around all the contestants."

"Do you miss your roommate?" he asked.

Recently, Vivian had been the eighth chef to be sent home. "I do. She was funny and I could count on her to lighten the mood. I'm not looking forward to being alone in my room."

"If this afternoon goes well, perhaps I'll ask to be your new roommate."

"You will do no such thing. I don't want to be gossiped about."

"Why does gossip bother you so much?" he asked. "That's the second time you've mentioned it."

"It bothers everyone. No one wants to hear their name whispered behind their backs."

"We aren't doing anything wrong," he said.

"I know. But I'd rather keep it private," she said. "Between us." She couldn't help but admit that if for some reason her track record with men held true and Remy ended up breaking her heart and leaving her, she didn't want the cast of *Premier Chef* to know she'd been burned by love. Again.

9

REMY NEEDED A BREAK FROM the intense competition but
he also needed time alone with Staci. He'd been cooking at the top of his game, although that was due more
to the fact that she made him happy. She made him want
to be a better man and a better chef. He cherished the
moments they had spent together.

Like on a Quick Cook when they had brushed hands
while reaching for the same bunch of basil. Or when he'd
met her gaze as she'd turned to put a pot on the stove.
Or a million little instances that had been not enough
for him. He wanted to see if it were simply the fact that
he couldn't have her that was making everything about
her seem so enchanting.

And this day was for them. He'd had to use his credit
card to book the yacht and though he didn't like leaving
a trail for his parents to follow and perhaps find him,
he'd needed to do it for himself and for Staci. He wanted
to show that he was more than an out-of-work cook and
this type of a day was something he could offer her.

Staci stretched out on one of the loungers to tan and

he stood next to her his hands actually tingling as he anticipated touching her back. She handed him the sunscreen but all he could do is stare down at her. The black bikini bottoms hugging the curve of her butt beckoned him. He sat down next to her on the bench, stroking his hand down her left leg. She lifted herself on her elbows and glanced over her shoulder at him.

"I don't feel any lotion," she said.

"Are my hands too rough? I know I have calluses and scars. You should be touched by something as soft as you are," he said.

"Your hands are fine. I was teasing you. Touch me if you want. But I will burn so I have to put lotion on."

"I'll make sure you're covered. I never burn," he said.

"Thanks to your olive skin. I wish I had it. I'm so pale. I could stand in the sun for hours and never get any color other than red."

He smiled at her. He wouldn't change anything about her body. The soft pale skin was part of Staci. He poured lotion onto his hand and warmed it by rubbing his hands together and then stroked his hand down her left leg. He started at the curve of her butt and then worked his way slowly down the back of her thigh. She giggled when he reached the back of her knee.

"Ticklish?"

"Not normally. I think I'm nervous to have you touching me while I just lie here."

"Surely you must have some fantasy of being massaged by a man who has to put only your pleasure first," he said. He was having a few fantasies of being just such a man for her.

"Well, yes, but is that what you're doing?"

"Yes. I am. I told you the sex we had was nice but it left me craving more. I still don't know your body or you." He kept moving his hand in tiny circles on the back of her knee. She shifted a little to turn and face him.

"I don't know you either," she said.

"I promise you will." It was impossible to learn a woman the way he needed to know her without revealing at least something of himself. And though he was a man living a lie he knew he wanted her to know him. He needed that kind of sexual honesty between them now and, he suspected, for the future.

"Okay. I'm going to lie here and let you be my personal masseur."

"Perfect," he said. He put more lotion on his hands and finished moving slowly down her leg. He took a minute to massage her calf knowing that being on her feet all day would make those muscles ache. It wasn't guesswork; he'd had the same aching legs at the end of a long day cooking.

"That feels good," she said. "Last year for Christmas, Alysse and I went to the Spa at the Hotel Coronado and had massages…"

"How do I measure up?" he asked, letting his hands slide between her legs and sweep up to the apex of her thighs.

"You are a bit more…intimate," she said.

"I should hope so," he said, not liking the thought of another man's hands on her. He knew that jealous wasn't noble and tried to shove it aside but he wanted Staci to be his. And his alone.

There was something about Staci that made him possessive. Maybe it was that he was away from Gastrophile, which consumed every second of his life when he was home. Or maybe it was just Staci. It was too early in knowing her to make that determination. He only knew that there was something about her that had captured him.

He poured more lotion in his other hand, starting at the top of her right thigh and slowly moving his way down to her feet. She had tiny feet. And delicately painted toe-nails, he lifted her leg and rubbed the lotion into each foot before caressing his way back up the inside of her legs. He admitted to himself that caress was for himself, but noticed that she shifted slightly, parting her legs, and he guessed she liked his touch, too.

"I'll do your back and then you roll over and I'll do your front," he said.

"Hmm…mmm…."

He couldn't tell if it was sleepiness that made her mutter that sound or just the simple enjoyment of being touched. He poured more lotion on his hands and starting at the waistband of her bikini bottoms placed his hands on her back. He spread his fingers wide and moved them in slow circles upward. He noticed that one of his hands could span her waist as he rubbed his hands over her.

There was a small mark in the middle of her back just above her waist and he leaned closer to check out the strawberry colored mark, brushing hands over and over it. Some sort of birthmark, he thought.

"The only part of my back that has color," she said. "I can't wear low cut dresses."

"Why not?"

"Everyone always thinks I have something on my back," she said.

"Everyone or men?" he asked, knowing that if he saw her in a slinky dress and noticed a mark on her back he'd be desperate to touch it and her.

She thought about it and then shrugged. "Mostly men."

"Yeah, they want to touch you, *ma chère*."

"I don't let them," she said. There was something very private about her. He imagined that was because she didn't let people in very easily. He wanted to be let in, he thought.

"I'm glad," he said and meant it.

He caressed the centerline of her spine, careful not to rub too hard. Finally he reached the back fastening of her bikini top and he deftly undid it as he continued to massage her back. He really liked touching her. He couldn't believe they'd made love and this was the first time he was seeing her beautiful back and really taking the time to enjoy touching her.

"Um…what are you doing?"

Turning himself on, he thought, shifting his legs as his erection grew. "Making sure you don't burn," he said. "Your top could shift while you are lying here and I did give you my word that I wouldn't let you burn."

"Yes, you did," she said. "Your word means that much to you."

He shifted around so he could see her eyes because

there would be a time when she might doubt it, yet his word meant everything to him. "It does."

She looked at him intently and then reached over to touch his lips with her forefinger, tracing the lines of his mouth. "I want to believe everything you say but it's hard, Remy. It's not that I can't trust you...I can't trust myself."

FOR SOME REASON SHE DID trust Remy. Maybe it was the way he seemed to take everything in stride or maybe it was the fact that so far he hadn't been anything but honest with her. Or maybe it was those stupid feelings in her stomach that made her want to believe that he really cared for her.

She knew it was too soon to be love. But she also knew she was lying to herself. She'd never felt this way before. And maybe that had been why her cooking had suffered. All she thought about was Remy.

His hands on her back were turning her on but it was really just him stoking a fire that was already smoldering. A fire that had been growing with every slight touch in the *Premier Chef* kitchen. Each night as he slipped into her dreams. Every single morning when she saw him over coffee and regretted that they hadn't passed the night in each other's arms.

His hands moved smoothly over her back and down to her sides, his big fingers caressing the sides of both of her breasts, massaging gently but there was no way she'd confuse him with a masseuse and they both knew it. She savored every intimate second of it. Until she remembered that there was something almost too good to be true in Remy. She wanted to believe him—really there was nothing she wanted more in the world.

When he slipped his hands up to her shoulders and kneaded them she closed her eyes and wished she didn't have her past.

"You're tensing up."

"Sorry."

"What are you thinking?" he asked.

"That you can't be real. So far you haven't done anything wrong," she said.

"I lost the first two rounds," he said.

"Not in the competition," she said. But maybe that was what she should be thinking about. It was clear that his mind wasn't really on this peaceful afternoon away from the show. Though the sun was warm and his touch on her back even hotter, she felt a cold chill overtake her.

"Oh. Well in that case, I would have not slept with you that first night. I wish I'd waited until now so I could really know you."

"That's not a misstep. I wanted you to."

"I know that, but by taking you I let you believe I'm like every other man you've ever known. I made our getting to know each other even more difficult than it should be. Relax and let me make it up to you."

She wanted to. Finally she just ignored her nagging conscience. She was going to enjoy this time with Remy. Even if he turned into a two-headed toad after this she'd have these moments. And she'd cherish them. No man had done this for her. No man had cooked for her. No man had treated her the way Remy did.

That had to count for something. She felt something

warm and damp tease her neck and realized he was kissing her. Goose flesh spread out from the place where he was nibbling on her shoulder. Her breasts felt heavier and her nipples tightened.

She felt his mouth moving along her back in the same path his hands had taken. He lingered over her shoulder blades and then he encouraged her to move her arms above her head. He shifted over her and she felt his chest hair against her back.

Then she felt the tender warmth of his breath. He touched the curve of her breast. His other hand caressed her nipple. Her hips jerked and his hand slid down to her butt, to one cheek.

His mouth slowly left a trail of nibbling kisses. "You're so beautiful, *ma chère*. I love touching you."

She wanted to say she loved being touched by him but the words stuck in her throat. Ultimately, she didn't want to reveal to him what she felt. She was more afraid of him in this moment than she had been in any other. There was something scary about letting him see how much he affected her. She didn't want him to know that he had this kind of power over her. But she knew it was more than likely too late to stop it.

He kissed the side of her right breast and he did that thing where he swept his finger under her body and over her nipple again. She moaned his name. Hoping she appeared nonchalant but knowing there was no way to hide her body's reaction to him, especially when he sweetly stroked between her legs.

She was determined to appear cool and in charge, even though she knew she wasn't cool at all. She was sizzling in the summer sun. And there was nothing that was going to make her cool off.

When he reached her feet he licked the arch of one foot then the other before again working his way up the inside of her leg. Oh, God, his mouth moved closer to her center and everything inside of her clenched. Afraid of what he might not do, or where he might not go.

At her very core, he left a little kiss and started his journey down that leg.

She was a mass of quivering nerves and barely aware of when he put his hands on her waist and rolled her to her back.

"I think we made sure you are not going to get burned on your back…now to make sure your front is okay."

"You are taking this seriously," she said, not at all surprised that her voice sounded husky and low.

"That's the kind of man I am. How are you liking your massage so far?" he asked.

She tried to seem calm when she shrugged but the fabric of her loosened bikini top started to slide and she had to grab for it. "It's good."

He smiled at her. "I'm glad."

He poured lotion in his hands and started again at the top of her thigh working his way down to her feet. This time was worse because she could see his face as he touched her body. He did seem to enjoy every inch of her skin. And there was a part of her that knew she'd never forget that look.

It was easy to believe that he was as involved in her as she was in him except for the rapt way he looked at her body. He glanced up and saw her watching him.

"What?"

"I just didn't believe you really wanted me…I mean in more than a sexual way until now. Any other guy would have been after his own satisfaction, but not you."

"Oh, I intend to have satisfaction and much more, but you're a mystery to me, *ma chère*, and I'm not going to rush one thing with you."

REMY WASN'T USUALLY A patient lover. That was when it hit him that this was nothing like those vacation flings he'd had in the past. Yes, he was away from his normal life and he had the sun on his back. But Staci was the woman lying in front of him. He had never wanted a woman more. Her taste was on his lips, the imprint of her body was on his fingers and he longed to rip off that brief bikini bottom and bury himself hilt deep inside her.

She stared up at him with those clear gray eyes of hers and he knew that he didn't want to disappoint her in any way. There was vulnerability in her gaze that he knew she'd hate if she knew it was there.

He put his hands on her waist and leaned down to kiss her because he didn't want to face that clear gaze of hers for another second. He lingered over her mouth. Slowly, he pushed his tongue over her lips and teeth and tasted the hidden recesses of her mouth. Her taste was addictive. He couldn't imagine a time when he wouldn't want to be able to taste her. He needed her like a dying man needed to breathe.

Her hands came up to his shoulders and she clung to him while their tongues dueled and her body lifted toward his. He was ready for her, ready to take her but he'd meant what he'd said about wanting them to be in a bed the next time they made love, so he lifted his head and got to his feet.

"I think we've had enough sun for now," he said, his voice was gruff, his mind full of images of the two of them entwined on that big bed down in the stateroom. He'd made sure everything was ready for them before they'd left the marina. When he made love to her he wanted everything to be perfect.

She nodded, nibbling on her lower lip. He wanted to groan and couldn't help but steal another deep kiss. There was something about this woman that he couldn't get enough of.

"Definitely enough sun."

He lifted her into his arms; she was so slight that he carried her easily across the deck and down the few stairs to the stateroom. He closed the door behind them and placed her in the center of the queen-size bed. The light streamed through the sheer curtains on the port-hole windows.

She stretched her arms and legs out, letting the richness of the satin duvet caress her skin. The bikini top shifted around her breasts, showing him more of the pale white globes that he wanted to touch. She noticed his eyes stayed on her breasts and she reached up to undo the top knot behind her neck.

"Like what you see?" she asked. Her thick black bangs, falling in a heavy wave toward her eyes.

"You know I do," he said.

The fabric was still there just draped over her and he pushed his swim shorts to his ankles freeing his erection. He noticed that her gaze tracked down his body and paused on his masculinity. He took her ankles in his hands and drew her legs apart, before placing one knee between them. He reached for her bikini bottoms and pulled them down her legs, tossing them on the floor next to his swim trunks. Then he started kissing her legs again, starting at her feet this time.

He wanted to go as slowly as he had up on deck but his body had different ideas. He liked foreplay because the longer he drew out their coming together the more intense the feeling was when finally he was inside her body. But this was Staci and he felt as if it had been ages since he'd had her in his arms.

When he reached the top of her thighs he settled between her legs and parted her intimate flesh. With his tongue he flicked at the swollen bud there as her hips raised off the bed and into his touch. He kept flicking his tongue over and over that spot until she reached for him. The taste of her was spicy and he couldn't get enough of her. He teased and tempted her center until he felt her hips moving more quickly and her heels dug into the bed as her orgasm washed over her.

He was so hard he felt as if he were going to explode and when she reached down and took him in hand he almost did. He pulled her hand from him and drew her arm up and over her head.

He pushed aside the bikini top that revealed her hard pink nipples. Her breasts were small but curvy. They fit her tiny frame. He rubbed his hips over hers, letting the tip of his manhood settle into her while he suckled one nipple. He swirled his tongue over her engorged flesh until she shifted her shoulders and dug her hands into his hair to hold his head to her breast.

She chanted his name under her breath, the words were music to his ears, inflaming his desire and pushing him over the edge. He could barely hold on when he shifted to kiss and suck her other breast.

Her fingers tightened around his hair, but he wouldn't be hurried. Now that the end was so close he wanted her to enjoy every second of it. This time felt more real than their hurried coupling on the balcony had. This was what he'd been waiting for since he'd met her.

He stopped to look up at her. Her lips were parted, her eyes were half closed. Her hands flung above her head with abandon and her skin was covered in a dark pink flush. He memorized her in this instant before he thrust a final time into her.

She cried out as they climaxed together. She wrapped her legs around his waist and kept him buried inside her.

He wanted to give Staci everything he had. And he realized that she was more important to him than any other woman he'd ever been with.

He rolled to his side, keeping their bodies joined but held his weight from crushing her. A sense of peace and belonging overcame him, although he knew that it wouldn't last because no matter what he'd been trying to tell himself this wasn't real. He wasn't even the man she thought he was.

10

STACI STRETCHED, ROLLED over and curled against Remy.
There was no confusion about where she was or whom
she was with. And for the first time since she'd left
Paris all those years ago, she felt as if she hadn't made
a mistake in trusting a man. She snuggled closer to him,
breathing in the woodsy scent of his aftershave, the lingering smell of sea breeze on his skin and the subtle
fragrance of sex.

He squeezed her tight and rubbed his hand down her
back in a long languid stroke. It occurred to her that if
they stayed here at sea for the rest of their lives everything would be okay. It was only when they got around
others that they'd encounter problems. But her grandmother had always warned her about hiding from the
truth.

There was a reason she wanted to hide and that was…
she didn't know. Maybe she was scared or too attached
to Remy. Maybe she didn't want him to know that he
could make her feel as good as he had. Because she still
was afraid to really trust him. She might feel good now,

but her mind was getting active and her doubts floated to the fore.

Tension settled over her and stole her sunshine as sure as clouds could on a summer's day.

"What are you thinking about?"

"Getting up," she said, because that was the safest answer.

"Yeah, right. Come on, what are you really thinking? You owe me that."

She realized he had a point. She just wasn't sure she could tell him. She just didn't know if she could drop her baggage at the door and be the woman that could make a relationship work with Remy.

"If you could see your face," he said.

"What would I see?" she asked.

"A woman who's afraid."

Exactly as she feared but she'd always known she didn't have a poker face. She didn't have it in her to be false with people once she started caring about them. No matter how much she wanted to deny it, she did care for Remy.

"I keep circling around and coming back to the same spot about trusting you," she said. "But right now I have to protect myself—"

"No you don't. We're in this together, you and me. We don't have to protect ourselves from each other."

She pulled the sheet up with her as she sat next to him. Tucking her hair behind her ear, she stared at him through narrowed eyes. "I can only assume you've never had a broken heart."

He shrugged in that Gallic way of his and it wasn't so

charming to see his casual attitude when she was feeling everything way too intensely.

"I tend to keep things casual because that's my way. My job is pretty demanding."

"Yes, but you're between gigs now. So what's keeping things so low-key this time?" she asked.

"We're away, in a different place," he said. "It's not the norm."

She arched both eyebrows at him and he shook his finger at her. "Don't get your back up. You know damned well you wouldn't have looked twice at me if we weren't trapped here together. This show is giving us a reprieve from our everyday lives. It's your chance to trust in a man and mine to slow down."

"What happens when this reprieve is over?" she asked, fearing she already knew his answer. Remy was the kind of guy who could move on. She had to remember his words. They weren't in the real world right now. She couldn't fall in love with a man who was enjoying a vacation from his life.

"I don't know, *ma chère*. I don't have all the answers. I didn't expect to meet you or to feel the way I do about it, but there it is whether I want it or not. If I could walk away from you then the last two weeks would have been a stroll in the park."

She didn't say anything.

"For both of us. Denying it won't change the truth. There is something between us that we can't deny. You know it's true or you wouldn't have been so tense the last two weeks."

He had a point but she hated it. She didn't want him

to be right or for this situation to be out of her control. Yet it had been since she'd tripped over the threshold of the elevator and fell into his arms.

He'd caught her and she had to wonder if that's why she thought she could trust him. If that's why she really wanted to make this work.

She hated the weakness inside her that made it impossible for her not to hope that...well, that this would last. "Let's stop talking about it."

"Why? You'll keep worrying over it, won't you?"

"Yes. But talking isn't making it any better," she said.

"It is, *ma chère*. It's letting you know that you're not alone. I'm unsure, too," he said.

"Renting a yacht and seducing me on the sun deck doesn't seem unsure to me."

He tugged her off balance and back into his arms. "I wanted to show you I was more than just a one-night kind of guy."

She had to laugh because there was no way that she'd ever have thought that about Remy. Even their first intense lovemaking hadn't felt casual. Nothing did with him and she knew if she didn't want to go crazy she would have to start forgetting the fear that he wasn't a man of his word.

After all everything he'd done since they'd met had proven to her that he wasn't lying about his feelings.

"What else do you have planned for today?"

"I was hoping we'd cook together in the galley. I've ensured that we have state-of-the-art appliances. Then we'll eat on the deck under the moonlight, maybe dance to some Cajun rock and then I'll seduce you again before we go back to the house."

"I can see you've given this some thought."

"I have," he said. "I wanted...I still want to get to know the woman behind all these defenses, Staci. I care about you. I can't make myself stop thinking about you."

She understood what he was saying; he was verbalizing what she felt. She knew if she kept her guard down then she could enjoy the rest of her time with him. And to be fair it would probably be easier on him; he could stop worrying that he wasn't living up to her needs.

"Okay but I'm in charge in the kitchen."

"Like you were the first time," he said.

"Ha. This time you take orders and act as my sous chef," she said, standing up and reaching for her bikini bottoms.

"As you wish," he said.

"As if. You'll let me think I'm in charge, won't you?"

"You bet," he said with a grin. "Let's shower and I took the liberty of stocking some clothing for you."

"You did?" she asked. "Who does that?"

"A man who wants to impress his woman."

His woman. Was she really Remy Stephens's woman? Did she want to be? She knew she did. That was why she was laboring over everything he said and did. She wanted this to be real. More real than she'd wanted her father to show up when she was a kid. It was wrong in a way that a man still held the key to her happiness and she was afraid to let him see how much he meant to her.

"Well, I'm impressed," she said. "Are we showering together?"

"No, I'll let you have the facilities first. I need to check with the captain and tell him we won't be fishing," he said.

"I doubt you ever really intended for us to do that," she said.

"Why?"

"I think you said it so I wouldn't be wondering if you were going to make a play for me."

"You're right. I wanted you to relax. And I think I succeeded."

He had done that all right. "Thank you, Remy."

"For what?"

"The massage, the understanding. I know it's been difficult—"

"Nothing worth having comes easily," he said, before he pulled on his swim trunks and walked out of the stateroom.

STACI REGAINED HER equilibrium in the kitchen while Remy showered. She chopped vegetables, letting the sounds of her knife on the cutting board sooth her. The captain and crew were still staying out of sight, which Staci truly appreciated. She felt raw and exposed after making love with Remy and needed to put herself back together.

She was used to always being the strong one, the one who was tough and made everyone else feel better. Even Alysse let her be the tough one. It was Staci who always dealt with difficult small business loan officers, overzealous customers and one time a would-be burglar.

At this moment she felt entirely incapable of doing anything but working in the kitchen.

"What can I do?" Remy asked as he came and stood beside her.

He wore a pair of jeans and a white linen shirt that he'd left unbuttoned at the neck. His hair was still damp from the shower and the white linen made his skin tone seem even deeper. Seeing him now she wondered how a man as together and successful as Remy could be out of work. He seemed more like a wealthy restaurant owner.

"I wasn't sure what we were making so I'm just chopping vegetables," she said. "I already made some cupcakes for dessert...they're baking in the oven."

"Cupcake girl, I'm flattered," he said, and dropped a kiss on her neck. "Face me so I can see if the dress I ordered looks as lovely on you as it did on the model."

She put her knife down. She thought this was part of the problem, too. She normally wore jeans and a T-shirt. The dress was a simple sundress that tied at the back of her neck. The skirt fell to her knee and wasn't full or flowy, something which would have made her petite frame seem shorter. He'd chosen well, she thought. But now that he was standing there waiting to see how she looked she was nervous.

To heck with it, she thought. She'd never been a nervous Nelly why was she behaving like one now?

She turned toward him and put her hands on her hips, staring up at him in challenge. "What do you think?"

He tipped his head to the side and peered at her for what seemed like an eternity. "Exquisite. But why are you angry?"

"I don't know. This isn't me. I'm jeans not fancy dresses. And this place is nice but it's outside my comfort zone."

"I'm sorry. I thought you'd enjoy a vacation from everything."

"The house in Malibu is that as well. I feel like this is just one more illusion," she said. Knowing she meant her feelings. There was something inside of her that was so scared and unsure. And every move that Remy made just reinforced how out of control she really was.

"This is real," he said. "Even though I'm out of work right now I have money."

That knocked her back. Yet it made perfect sense. He was totally at ease in any situation. It was something that she'd noticed in wealthy friends before. "Oh, okay."

"Staci, we are getting to know each other in carefully measured steps. You and I are creating a new dish and every time we get something right and try to move onto the next ingredient we have to readjust."

She agreed. "I'm not wealthy, but the cupcake business has been good to me and Alysse. We have an investor interested in expanding Sweet Dreams into a chain of stores. If that happens, we'll both be millionaires."

"Good to know. Are you going to do it?"

Staci shrugged. "I'm not sure. I have been considering doing other things, but we're both just so used to bakery…what would we do without Sweet Dreams."

"I'm sure any new investor would love it if you both stayed on and worked there," he said, coming over next to her and taking over chopping the vegetables.

"But we would be working for someone else. That doesn't seem right."

He laughed at her and she smiled back. "I know I'm bossy, what can I say?"

They worked together making a seafood gumbo that she'd been dying to try and with his input she thought it tasted very nice. When the cupcakes had cooled she set them on the countertop next to the icing she'd prepared.

"So we can decorate our own or decorate one for each other," she said.

"I vote for each other. What do you have here?"

"Buttercream frosting, fondant, colored sugar...the usual suspects," she said. Handing him an offset spatula.

"Is there a theme?" he asked.

"I think you've been a *Premier Chef* too long. It's a dinner date, southern man. You make whatever you want," she said.

"You're right. Okay, prepare to be amazed," he said.

"I've been amazed all day," she admitted. "I think I was so grumpy earlier because I'd thought I'd figured you out, but once again you've made me re-evaluate you."

"Good," he said. "You're still a big ol' mystery to me, *ma chère*. No matter how much I think I know you I keep realizing I don't."

She was glad. She didn't want to think that Remy had uncovered too many of her secrets. There were parts of her that even she didn't want to know. They each took a cupcake to the galley table and sat down at opposite ends. She worked with food coloring and the different frostings to do an image of Remy on top of her cupcake. She'd won several awards for her artistic designs and she thought he'd be impressed. She used an upside down bowl to hide the cupcake, so he couldn't see the finished product until dessert time.

He took another bowl and put his cupcake in it. It had been hard but she'd resisted the temptation to look over at him several times while he'd been working. Finally they cleaned up the galley. Remy's watch pinged and he glanced down at it.

"It's almost time. I'll get the crew to finish prepping our dinner and bring it up to the deck while we have a cocktail and watch the sun set."

"Sounds good," she said. And it did. Everything Remy said sounded just right. Soon they were on deck French martinis in hand, the Chambord flavored cocktail just right as a light breeze stirred around them.

She shivered and Remy wrapped an arm around her shoulder. They sipped their drinks as the sun slowly drifted down and disappeared beyond the horizon. The deck wasn't dark for a second as twinkle lights came on and she heard the footsteps of the crew bringing their dinner up on deck.

It was a simple meal but she had seldom enjoyed one more. Remy talked to her more about his travels and the people he'd met. But he did it in such a way that she didn't feel envious or jealous. They talked about Paris and Staci felt that bittersweet pang she always did, but it faded as Remy and she compared favorite sites and meals they'd had there.

She was afraid to admit it even to herself but she knew as the meal ended and the slow, sexy music began, that she was falling in love with him. He pulled her into his arms and danced her around the deck under the moon. She rested her head on his shoulder, sure that this one night she could let him see that she wasn't always a tough cookie.

Sure that she could allow herself to enjoy the moonlight, the man and the memories that felt as if they'd last forever. But being Staci she couldn't help but worry that tomorrow there would be another surprise like his wealth. That niggled at the back of her happiness, stealing a little of it. What if the next thing she found out about him wasn't as pleasant as this one?

REMY WAS RELUCTANT TO leave the yacht. He wasn't a man who normally hid from life, so today had been a refreshing change from the persona he'd been maintaining for the last few weeks. But he also knew that showing Staci he was a wealthy man was a far cry from telling her the truth about who he was.

He was doing all he could to prepare her for the truth once it came out. The more he cooked and the way things had gone lately, he was pretty sure he could win this thing. And when he did, and the episodes started to air his real name would be revealed.

"Thank you for a wonderful day," she said, wrapping the Hermès scarf he'd given her around her shoulders.

"You're welcome." He felt so sure of himself with her that if it weren't for the lie of his identity, he'd already have swept her off to his Garden District mansion in New Orleans.

Even if that were possible Staci wouldn't blindly go

where he wanted her to go. He admired her strength and independence. A part of him feared these six weeks in Malibu might be all the two of them ever had together.

"We haven't had dessert," she said.

"You are right. I'm having coffee brought up and then we can sit on the deck and enjoy our dessert."

The staff brought a silver coffee service and placed a cup in front of each of them. Then their dishes with cupcakes were set on the table. Remy was the first to admit he didn't know anything about decorating cakes. They had a head pastry chef at Gastrophile—his cousin Helene who was a genius at desserts, but he'd wanted to impress Staci.

Did he always? There was something about her...or maybe it was something about him and the fact that he knew he couldn't be totally truthful with her, that made him strive to always impress her.

She smiled as she handed him her covered cupcake. "Open it."

"Okay," he said, and then sat staring at the cupcake. She'd captured his likeness on the small dessert. It was amazing and a little bit unnerving. "I'm supposed to eat my own face?"

She laughed. "I know it's weird. You can lift the fondant off and save it, if you can't do it."

"Why haven't you made a dessert in the competition?" he asked. "You have a lot of talent."

"I know I do. But there hasn't been an appropriate task for it yet. If there is, I'll try my best to win."

"I'm pretty sure you will win hands down," he said.

"Now, open mine. Keeping in mind I'm not a pastry chef."

She gave him one of those enigmatic looks of hers from under eyelashes. "Are you nervous? Say it isn't so, southern man. I thought you had ego to spare."

"I do, but I'm also a realist and let's face it I don't have your skills at dessert."

She raised the makeshift lid and caught her breath. She slowly lifted the cupcake out and set it on the plate in front of her. "You made me a water lily."

"Yes, I did. It wasn't until dinner that I learned you liked Monet. So I think we are going to have to put this down to really good chemistry between us."

She reached over and took his hand as she looked up at him with those pretty gray eyes of hers. "It's perfect. And I don't think you should worry about any dessert rounds in the competition."

"As long as I can do something simple I'll be okay," he said. But he didn't want to talk about *Premier Chef*. He wanted this day and night to be about them. "Do you really like it?"

She lifted his hand to her mouth and kissed his knuckles before letting it go. "Yes, I do."

They ate their desserts both of them lingering over them.

"Why did you do my cupcake like that?" he asked.

"Something to remember me by," she said, glancing over at him.

He met her gaze. It seemed as if time itself was standing still. He wasn't a romantic, not really, but tonight he thought he could be. "I'd rather have you instead of having to remember you."

Something flickered across her face and she looked away before turning back to him with a tight smile. "But we both know I won't last. With you."

"Why?" he asked, afraid he knew the answer. Still, he wanted to hear it from her own lips. He wanted to have a chance to defend himself. To show her he was different from the other men in her life. But then he was afraid that no matter how different he was his outcome in her life might be the same. He was determined it wouldn't be.

"You said it earlier. The *Premier Chef* house is an illusion. Win or lose we are both going back to our real lives. And I live here. My friends and family are here and I'm not sure I'd ever really trust you enough to give that up."

"What if I were the one who gave up New Orleans?" he asked.

"Would you?" she asked. Then she shook her head. "I don't know. That's a lot to put on a relationship. If you moved out here and things didn't work out...I think it's more likely that this is a sweet affair that will end when the competition does."

He sat back in his chair and crossed his arms over his chest. He knew he should say something to lighten the mood. He didn't want the day to end on a sour note, but he couldn't accept her version of things. He knew she was right, he thought, that was why it made him so angry that she had put it so plainly. Because she didn't know who he was and that leaving New Orleans was impossible for him.

"I never pegged you for a quitter. I've seen you bring dishes back from the edge that should have been thrown away," he said. "Why would you live your life with less passion?"

She put her napkin on the table after folding it carefully. "Food hasn't ripped my heart out."

"I haven't either," he said.

"Not yet," she said, getting to her feet.

He almost let her go but he couldn't. And that was the part that bothered him. He wasn't willing to say this was just an affair, a part of him wanted more with this complex and sexy woman.

He stood up quickly, knocking his chair over in the process. She stopped and turned back to him.

"Remy—"

"Don't say it. I'm not going to hurt you. I've promised you I wouldn't. True, there are things about me you don't know. But everything I have shown you…it's more than I've given any other woman. I'm not playing a game with you, Staci."

He picked the chair up and stood to see if she'd left but instead she'd come back to his side. "You frighten me. I can't be as open to this as you are. I know that's not fair but that's what life has taught me."

He tugged her into his arms because he was very much afraid no matter how well he prepared her now, when the truth was revealed about him it would hurt her greatly. If he was a stronger man—a better man— he knew he would have let her walk away.

And since he only had these six weeks in Malibu he was determined to make them the best six weeks of her life.

11

WHEN THEY ARRIVED AT the house, there was no time for a long goodbye, which was fine, Staci thought. Jack was waiting in the living room with two of the other finalists, Christian and Will.

"What's up?" Remy asked as they settled into chairs.

"A special announcement," Jack replied. "We're waiting for the last few contestants to show up. By the way, did you enjoy your day off?" Jack asked them.

Staci would have liked to have gotten changed and been in her normal jeans and T-shirt in front of the other competitors. She didn't want them to see her dressed up and it was making her uncomfortable.

"It was very nice and relaxing," she said, hoping she was playing it cool. "Can I go change?" she asked the producer.

"No, I'm sorry you can't," Jack said.

"Just be glad you weren't skate boarding all day and smell like sweat," Christian remarked.

Everyone laughed at the way he'd spoken. Staci noticed Remy's hands resting on his knees. She so wanted to reach out to him to remind her of his touch.

Eventually, the rest of the group arrived and when they were all seated in the living room Jack stood up. "Now that we've reached the halfway point in the contest we will be upping the stakes. Cars will be here for you at six tomorrow morning. You will all need to pack your bags and bring along your formal wear—men that's suits and ties for you, ladies that's dresses. We are taking you to New York City. I suggest you get a good night's sleep because you will hit the ground running with a Quick Cook as soon as you land."

"How long will we be in New York?" Remy asked.

"One week. We'll fly back here for Judges Table and Elimination on Friday night," Jack said. "So you don't have to pack everything."

"Will there be any guest judges?" Christian asked.

"Yes. But I can't give you any names. I will say this, there is more than one guest judge and they are both world famous. Any other questions?"

A million but none she thought she'd get the answers for tonight.

"Good. We'll see everyone in the morning. As always, good luck."

Jack left the room and as soon as he did there was muttering from everyone.

"New York…have you been back since the visit with your mother?" Remy asked her.

"No. Unless you count a stop-over when I flew to Paris. But I didn't leave JFK so I don't think anyone would count that," she said. She wondered who the guest judges would be but now that Jack was gone, she wanted to get back to her room and have some time alone.

"I was just there before I came out here to audition. Should be nice to be back there," he said.

"I'm sure it will be. I'm going to pack and get ready for bed," she said.

"I'll walk up with you."

She shook her head. "Gossip."

"Everyone here knows you two hooked up," Sarah called out. "It's no big deal and kind of sweet."

Staci groaned. "Fine. You can walk up with me."

Remy laughed but she knew his mind wasn't on this house. "Are you worried about New York?"

He shook his head. "Just not sure who the guest judges will be. It bothers me that they didn't tell us who they are."

"Why?"

"There are some chefs I'd rather not see," he said.

"Bad blood?" she asked. The gourmet cooking world was full of its share of…well, divas for lack of a better word. Prima donnas who'd always been told they were the best and had rarely heard the word no. In a way that was what Jean-Luc Renard had been. But Staci had been young and he'd been so passionate that she'd easily mistaken lust for love.

She was only now realizing how mistaken she'd been about her ex. The feelings that she had for Remy were a hundred times more powerful than those she'd had for Jean-Luc.

That should upset her more than it did. Remy seemed

distracted as he sat quietly in her room. Something was obviously bothering him.

"Sort of," he said at last. "I just don't know if I'm imagining trouble where there will be none or what."

That sounded vaguely ominous. She wondered what kind of trouble he was talking about and reminded herself she only knew about Remy based on what he'd told her. She wanted to believe he was the man he'd shown himself to be but what if he was doing something to fool her.

"Want to talk about it?" she asked. "I'm told that I am a really good listener."

"I can see that. One of the things I've noticed about you during the competition is how adept you are at helping the other contestants. And that comes from paying attention to people."

"Thanks for the compliment," she said. "That's also how I know what is going on with people. If you pay attention to people they can't shock you."

"Truly?" he asked. "Does that work?"

"Usually…so do you want to talk about whatever is on your mind?"

"No."

"Well that was definitive," she said. "I'd say that you are afraid of something or someone. Am I right?"

"Perhaps," he said. "But if that were true I'd never admit it to the one chef in this competition who could actually beat me."

"You think I could win?" she asked, interested to hear what he thought unguarded about her cooking. It was the one thing that she thought really defined her.

"Yes. You know you could, too."

She knew better than to get cocky. "Do you think you might lose?"

He sighed and ran his hands through his hair, tousling it and making the curls spike up before he smoothed them back into place. "I'm not sure, but I just don't like not knowing."

"I agree it's unnerving, which is probably why they did it. It's probably some chef who's friends with Hamilton," she said. "It'll probably be someone with a show on this network. You know how incestuous these things can be"

"Why are you so calm about it?"

She smiled at him. "Because you're not. Anything that rattles our current champ has to be good. Sort of levels the playing field for me."

"Brat," he said.

"Whatever. There is one thing I'm not looking forward to," she said, as her gazed strayed to Remy. It was hard to concentrate on anything other than him. He sat on the bed that had been Vivian's and though they were talking as friends, she could still sense their underlying physical chemistry.

"What is it? That we'll get stopped at airport security for trying to carry through our knives?" he asked, smiling.

"No, but that would be funny. You should totally go and tell Jack to consider it. We could cross promo with the cop show." She could just imagine Jack weighing the idea as if it were a serious option. She'd learned the producer spent most of his time analyzing ratings and trying to figure out how to get a bigger share of the audience. Hence him letting them leave the house for the day.

Remy laughed. "You're learning that this is all about ratings."

"Aren't you? It's all that they seem motivated by. The judges are here for the food and the cooking but the producers obviously want good TV."

"Yes, they do," Remy said, getting up and coming over to sit down next to her. "You were about to tell me what you weren't looking forward to."

That's right, she was. "Um...I kind of like having the upper hand on you. "

"I won't tell anyone whatever it is that's bothering you," he said.

"I don't like flying. Normally I'd take a travel sickness pill that would knock me out, but since Jack said we'd be doing a quick cook when we land..."

Remy reached for her hand and held it in his. "I'll be there next to you."

The words shouldn't have been as soothing as they were but she knew that if Remy were beside her she could succeed at anything.

REMY HELD STACI'S HAND as they sat next to each other on the bed and knew that it was time for him to tell her the truth about who he really was. He knew there was a pretty good chance that the guest judge in New York could end up being his uncle or one of his other assorted relatives.

He also had the feeling that he should go and talk to Jack about it, too. He didn't want his uncle to be waiting at the Quick Cook, see him and reveal who Remy actually was. He knew that good TV aside, that type of thing would really hurt Staci and probably his chances of winning the show.

But she curled next to him tucking her head on his shoulder and the very last thing he wanted to do was to disturb her. Yeah, right, he thought. Since when did he start lying to himself? Maybe this new persona was having a bad influence over him.

"Everyone was nice about us being a…"

"A couple?" he asked.

She nodded, but didn't say anything else. God, this woman with all her skepticism and trust issues needed a man who was honest with her. She couldn't even say they were in a relationship because it possibly wouldn't last and he was…well, he was just holding her and staying silent because he knew that if he mentioned his last name wasn't Stephens he'd lose her.

It was that simple. He could pretend that he'd told her enough truths about himself to make up for the one lie and that lie had been told before he'd ever even met her, but he knew that he was making excuses for himself. And they were excuses she wouldn't buy.

He shifted around on the bed so that he was leaning against the headboard with two pillows stacked behind his back and drew Staci into his arms. He couldn't help but notice that she actually let him and that she cuddled next to him so trustingly.

"Thanks for today."

"You already thanked me," he said. This day was going to be one he cherished for the rest of his life. In his mind this was the day he first made love to Staci. It had been more than sex and had changed him in many different ways. Prior to today he would have been able to keep up the illusion that he was just an out-of-work cook, but now he wanted her to know everything about him. Truly, he needed her to.

Because as he held her in his arms he acknowledged that he wanted her to be by his side for the rest of his life. Inside a part of him that had never been alive before awakened and he realized that he loved her.

Sleeping in here tonight, holding her in his arms, might be something he needed but another part of him knew that if he did that he'd lose all hope of protecting a part of himself that he'd never known was vulnerable before.

Until he came clean with Staci and told her all about Gastrophile. Until she knew everything about him and he about her he couldn't let her know how he felt. He wasn't completely sure if she'd return his emotions. As wary as she was of the opposite sex, a big part of him believed she'd never be able to forgive him.

And he had to figure out how to let her know who he really was and convince her that he hadn't really been lying to her the entire time they'd known each other. He shoved his newly realized feelings to the back of his mind, knowing that people who made decisions based on anything other than logic often regretted them.

When he left her room he'd call Jack and start the process of revealing who he really was.

"What are you thinking about?" she asked him.

"Cooking," he said and it was partially true. "I've never met anyone like you before."

"I didn't want to trust you, Remy, but a part of me can't help it. Every time I start to think you're lying to me about something you prove that you aren't…"

Her words were like a dagger in his heart and he knew if he were a braver man, a stronger man, he'd confess then and there. But he wasn't. He'd never seen this particular look in Staci's eyes before and when she gazed at him with all that trust and devotion, he couldn't help but want to bask in it. To want to pretend he was the man she thought he was.

Hell, he thought he was that man. At least, he had been until the show.

"You make me want to be better than I am."

"You've already proven yourself to be a man of honor," she said, touching his cheek softly and then leaning up to kiss him.

He deepened the kiss trying to show her with actions how much she meant to him and how deeply he cared for her. Even though he knew how he felt for her, the words were far away and hard for him to say.

"Please don't," he said at last.

"Don't what?"

"Make me sound like something I'm not," he said.

"What do you mean?" she said, pulling away to face him. "What is it that you aren't?"

He searched for a way to answer her. He knew that he was on shaky ground. "I'm not anything more than who I am."

"That's very zen of you," she said.

He sighed and rubbed his hand over his eyes. "I think I'm a bit tired."

"I know I am," she admitted. "What is it that you're trying to tell me?"

He took her hands in his and lifted each one to his mouth. He kissed the back of her hands and then drew her into his arms and squeezed her close. He didn't want to see the look in her eye right now because she seemed to see through the subterfuge and to the very heart of him.

"I care about you, *ma chère*. More than I have any other woman and that frightens me."

She squeezed him back, dropping a soft kiss on his neck before she glanced up at him.

"I care more for you than I have for any other man. In fact the only one who comes close almost ruined cooking for me. That's why I've been so recalcitrant with you."

"Recalcitrant? Really?" he asked, focusing on her personality instead of the fact that he might be responsible for doing the same thing to her and her passion for food. If he did ruin cooking for her, he'd never forgive himself.

"Okay fine, I've been stubborn and difficult. Alysse would say that's the only way I know how to be."

He could easily believe that. Since her nature was just contrary. "I think you're passionate."

"Ha. You say that now because I'm lying in your arms but I bet the last two weeks you thought of me differently."

"You're right, I did."

"See? But you've won me over. I can't help myself. I'm tired of fighting the both of us. If you can call us a couple, well, I guess I can, too."

He hugged her close as she stared up at him and he knew he needed to say something. Though the only words he had would be lies, so he kissed her and made love with her until the wee hours of the morning when she at last fell asleep and he snuck back to his room. He didn't call Jack or talk to anyone about his secret, but he felt like time was running out for him. And he only hoped he'd done enough to convince Staci that even though he'd been playing at being another man, the one he truly was adored her.

STACI WOKE ALONE AND that seemed to set the tempo for the entire morning. There was something distant about Remy though he was good to his word and held her hand during the flight take-off and landing. When they exited the flight and were out of the airport Fatima and Jack met them with two Escalades.

The crew were waiting for them as well and soon they were all miked and had make-up applied.

"Okay, guys, I hope you're all ready for some fun in The Big Apple," Fatima said. "You will be taken to the Time Square Marriott Marquis where you will drop your bags at the desk and have one hour to shop for food that represents the excitement of this trip and how you feel about having made it to the last half of the show.

"You will then have thirty minutes to cook your dish in the Marquis's convention kitchen. Are you ready to go?"

"Yes!" Staci shouted along with the other remaining contestants.

They were divided into groups, Remy in a different opposite one than she and then they headed to Times Square. They had been given directions to a Whole Foods market and sent to buy their ingredients. Staci tried to get close to Remy but he was in competition mode and she decided she should be, too.

She hadn't let him influence her this much since the first week of competition and she had decided that for the rest of the competition she would go back to making cooking her priority. She let the essence and vibe of the city sink into her soul as she walked to the grocery store and back. When she was in the kitchen and directed to her work station she started preparing her dish in her head. Going over each step in her mind since she'd only have thirty minutes to actually cook.

Fatima and Jack were there as they were all once again made presentable for the cameras and told to get ready to meet the guest judge. Staci hoped it was Bobby Flay or someone equally famous. She couldn't have been more shocked than when Jean-Luc Renard entered the kitchen. The guest judge was definitely someone she'd heard of.

She felt all the blood rush from her body and literally felt faint. Oh no, why hadn't she anticipated this?

Everyone was talking and she quickly raised her hand. "Jack, I need a minute."

"Cut," the director yelled.

Everyone was staring at her. She knew there was no

graceful way to do what needed to be done. Jack came over to her station but Jean-Luc had already noticed her.

"*Ma petite*, Staci. Good to see you again," he said in his slightly accented French.

"You know Chef Renard?" Jack asked.

"Yes. I'm sorry I wasn't sure if you needed to know that before we started cooking for this challenge," Staci said.

"Thanks for letting us know. I will talk to the other judges and our producers and get back to you. Everyone please go to the temporary green room," he said.

They all filed out of the kitchen and Staci was careful not to meet anyone's eyes, but as they reached the doorway, Remy took her arm and drew her to a halt.

"That's the man from your past?"

"Yes," she said.

"Why didn't you say?" he asked. "I was thinking your ex-lover was some—"

"Why does it matter?"

"Now I understand more what you meant by how he ruined cooking for you. Are you going to be okay cooking for him?"

"Yes," she said and realized it was true. A few weeks ago her answer might have been different but now all Jean-Luc was to her was an old boyfriend, nothing more. He didn't have the effect on her that he had previously. "I really am."

"Good. I'm still going to beat you," he said gesturing for her to enter the green room.

"I don't think so, southern man. I've got a dish planned that's going to blow the judges away."

"That's all well and good, Staci, but how do you know Chef Renard?" Quinn asked. "Doesn't seem fair if you have the advantage."

"I worked under him at his restaurant in Paris almost six years ago. We had a brief fling and I left," she said. It was easier for her to talk about the past if she just dealt it out in facts. No one would know that Jean-Luc had broken her heart when he'd dumped her to start an affair with the new pastry chef. Or at least, she hoped they wouldn't. It was hard enough to be on her A-game cooking against Remy—who she definitely had feelings for and knowing she'd be judged by Jean-Luc.

"Well, that's interesting," Whit said. "I guess you had more of a surprise than the rest of us when he walked through the door. I didn't even know who he was."

"He's one of the best chefs in the world," Staci said.

"Figures they'd get someone French. I think the next competition is going to be working in Ramsfeld's restaurant here," Christian said. "He's the only judge with a kitchen here. And his new menu is French cuisine inspired."

The door opened before anyone could comment and Jack stood there. "We need to see you, Staci."

She got up and followed Jack. She hoped they weren't going to penalize her for this. But really how could she have known that Jean-Luc would be asked to judge. She had noted on her experiences that she'd worked in Paris before opening her own bakery.

"Am I in trouble?" she asked.

"Not at all," Jack told her. "Chef Renard was a surprise and you couldn't have anticipated it. Fair enough.

The judges just want to talk to you before the Quick Cook."

She entered a small office where Fatima, Hamilton, Pete and Lorenz all waited. They gestured for her to have a seat.

"We've talked to Jean-Luc and he feels that he will not be biased against you in any way. Do you feel as if you could cook for him?" Lorenz asked.

"Yes. I don't feel as though having him for a judge will influence me one way or the other. It was a shock to see him," Staci acknowledged. "I just wanted to make sure you all knew that I'd worked for him."

"You did the right thing," Fatima said. "We will reveal the fact that you worked for him in a voice-over during the edited version of the show. How long has it been since you've seen him?"

"A little over six years," she said.

"Good. I think we're ready to get on with the competition," announced Hamilton. "Unless you have any further concerns, Chef Rowland?"

"I don't," Staci said.

"Good," Hamilton repeated. "Please go back and wait with your peers."

She nodded and did what he asked her to. The hallway was empty and Staci paused while she was still alone. Her bravado had seen her through this, but a tiny part of her felt betrayed all over again.

It made her appreciate Remy all the more. She was lucky to have him in her life. She stood a little taller as she walked down the hallway determined to put up a dish that made Chef Renard realize what a good cook she was, and possibly regret forcing her out of his kitchen all those years ago.

Her mind was focused on food as she re-entered the temporary green room. Remy waited just inside the door and took her hand in his, immediately squeezing it. Instantly she let go of all thoughts of the past instead focused on what was her future. She didn't need to cook to prove anything to Jean-Luc, she needed to cook for the joy of it. Cook for the new life that was waiting for her when this competition ended.

12

REMY DIDN'T MUCH CARE for the way that Chef Renard was preoccupied with Staci's dish. He knew the girl could cook, but Remy was a guy and he saw that the other man was flirting with Staci and perhaps regretting letting her go the way he had. He hoped the other man continued to regret it.

Staci appeared as if nothing was bothering her but Remy had felt her sweaty palms when they'd first entered the stew room after she'd seen her old lover for the first time. Frankly, Remy didn't admire Chef Renard. He'd been to his restaurant in Paris and his father Alain could cook a lot better than Jean-Luc.

"What have you prepared for us?" Fatima asked.

Remy described his dish and then stood back to let them taste it. He saw the other chef's eyes widen as the spice he'd used hit his palate. He knew that he had the other man in the palm of his hands. That he, Remy, had created a dish that was surprising the more experienced man. And in that moment, Remy knew that he wanted to best Chef Renard. To prove to Staci that he was the better man in every way.

But he couldn't do that as Remy Stephens. Remy Cruzel, however, cooked on the same level as Chef Renard.

"Very good. The taste is familiar to me," Renard said.

Remy just shrugged.

"Chef Stephens is from New Orleans and it is probably those seasonings that you are tasting," Fatima suggested. "Very nice."

Chef Renard gave him a quizzical look as they moved on to the next station and Remy wondered if he'd finally found a dish that would give him away. But then he knew he was tired of hiding. He wanted to come clean with Staci and the show so that he wouldn't feel like a liar and a cheat.

He was ready to claim his legacy now; he knew he could live up to his family's reputation whether or not he won the competition.

The reasons why he'd come, the need to show that he was ready to take on the role of Chef Patron had been assuaged. The last three weeks he'd cooked dishes in new ways and learned a lot about himself as a chef. He was proud of the cooking he'd done.

Fatima, Chef Renard and the other judges were back in the center of the room and as they looked over the stations, Remy couldn't help but notice that Renard avoided making eye contact with Staci.

"Okay, cut. Judges, you may go confer over your decision. Chefs, clean your stations."

They all started working and Remy cleaned his quickly and went to find Staci. He had some questions he wanted answers to. Not the least of which was what exactly had happened to end things between her and the other chef.

"Jack, how long is the break?"

"Fifteen minutes. The smokers are headed outside," Jack said.

"I'm going to take Staci up to the atrium for a chat," Remy said. "Is that okay?"

"Yes, be back on time," Jack warned.

"We will be."

"Who will be, what?" Staci asked coming up behind him.

"You and me back on time," Remy said, taking her hand in his and leading her away from the kitchen.

"We've got fifteen minutes, cupcake girl, and I want some answers," he said.

"Answers to what?" she asked. "I think I've done enough explaining about my past for the day. To be honest I'm ready to really put it behind me. I can't believe Chef Renard is going to be here all week."

Remy waited until they were alone on the escalator heading to the atrium. "Exactly what happened when you and Renard broke up?"

"Why does that matter?" she asked as he led the way to a padded bench hidden in a private alcove.

"I think he regrets it. Were you the one who ended things?" he asked as they were seated. He couldn't stand the thought that she might have ended it and now Renard might try to win her back.

She nibbled on her lower lip and looked up at him with an inscrutable gaze. She had her chef's coat on and because of the TV cameras she had on stage make-up, but underneath all that was the woman he knew very well. And he hated to see her looking so unsure.

"Why does that matter?" she asked.

"It matters because…," He hated this feeling, these emotions that made him feel vulnerable and ache inside. He wanted to just take her in his arms and never have to let her go. "Staci, he was looking at you like he was interested in rekindling your romance. So I want to know if that's a possibility?"

"No, Remy," she said. "There isn't a chance of that happening."

"Why not?" he asked. "If I lost you…well I'd always try to get you back."

"Really?" she asked, looking up at him this time with a very caring expression and he wondered if she had fallen for him too. He knew that she cared about him. She admitted that in spite of her fear of being lied to, she had started to believe in him.

"Yes," he said. "Did you really doubt it?"

"All I know is what I'm feeling," she said. "I know that you called us a couple, but I'm still not sure of myself to believe that this can last. So when you say things like that I'm a bit surprised."

"Why? You have to know what a lovely woman you are. Haven't I done enough to show you that?"

"You've done more than that, but it's my issue," she said. There was a wariness in her tone that told him she was exhausted from her past and how heavy a burden it must be for her to keep carrying it around. He wanted to take it from her but he wondered if he were really the man who could.

A part of him felt like she used the past as a wedge to keep him from getting too close and to keep her from really falling for him.

"Maybe it's time you let it go. Just because you've had a few bad relationships—"

"It's more than that, Remy. You asked me what happened with Jean-Luc and the truth is he moved on to another woman. I came into work one day and caught them together. That was it, he never said a word to me other than to say chefs had big appetites. I gave my notice and left."

"I'm sorry," he said.

"It's not your fault," she said, reminding him.

But he knew Staci. Proud, tough, confident Staci who had been hurt by that one incident. She'd been telling him all along that trust was going to come hard for her, but until now he hadn't realized just how hard. He had thought that he could just fix her hurt for her by showing her that a real man was tender and caring. But he saw now that the kind of betrayal she experienced, well...

Her past and his lie were pretty much kindred spirits and he knew, even though he'd been reluctant to admit it, that when the truth came out—and it would—Staci was going to walk away from him as surely as she'd left Jean-Luc Renard and Paris all those years ago.

STACI WON THE QUICK COOK, which made her feel satisfied. She knew she'd cooked well but more than that she was happy to know that Jean-Luc's praise meant nothing to her. It wasn't like the painful time when they'd been lovers and she'd waited and waited for some words of praise from him.

The fact that her reaction was no reaction showed her how much she'd moved on. Though she was used to keeping the past between her and Remy, she knew now that she was over it and really she only had one person to thank and that was her current lover.

The man who'd come in second in today's challenge. He winked at her across the studio when she'd been announced the winner and she knew he was proud of her achievement. What she liked about Remy was his own ability to give praise and not feel as if it stole anything from him. Jean-Luc hadn't been like that at all.

They were all told that Staci would have an advantage in the following day's elimination challenge and were sent one-by-one to record their video diaries about the day and the trip to New York. That night there would be a group dinner at Hamilton's restaurant, Ramsfeld East, and Staci suspected that Christian had been correct when he'd guessed that's where their challenge would be the next day.

They had the afternoon free.

"Want to go sightsee?" she asked Remy.

"That's the first time you've asked me on a date," he said.

"It'll be the last time too unless you answer correctly," she warned.

"Then, yes, I'd love to go with you. Where did you have in mind?" he asked.

"I've never been to the top of the Empire State Building," she said.

"You didn't go with your mom?" he asked, he'd hit all the touristy spots long ago with his parents and his cousins. And he hadn't been to the Empire State Building since he'd been twenty. As he stood there, thinking of all the places they could go, he finally realized that going back to New Orleans and cooking at Gastrophile was the only thing he really wanted.

"Mom was afraid of heights. Grandma and I decided we'd see a show with her instead of going up. But if you're game…"

"I am," he said. "Let's go."

When they got down to street level, Remy hailed a cab and gave the driver their destination. They sat in the back seat with the summer sun shining down on them.

"I can't believe you beat me today," Remy said. "I guess getting you to relax was a good strategy for you."

"It seems as if it was," she said with a cheeky grin. "To be honest. It's not being relaxed that is really the thing that made me win today," she said, full of mystery.

"I want to know what it is, but we're getting out at the end of the block," Remy said.

The cab stopped and Remy paid the driver. They followed the signs up to the ticket booth and then took the elevator to the viewing platform. Remy linked their hands together, realizing that even doing this type of thing was fun with Staci. He knew he needed to stop ignoring the truth that needed to be said but he couldn't.

"Okay, so tell me what made you win today," he said

after he'd led them to a spot away from most of the tourists.

"The truth?"

"Isn't it always about the truth with you?"

"Yes, it is," she said. Then she sighed and the breeze ruffled her short black hair. "It was knowing that you were the man you are…that sounds silly, doesn't it? But it was you and the way you made me feel. I channeled that into my cooking.

He was glad to hear it, he wanted to give her as much as he could so that she'd remember the good times with him when the bad inevitably came. Today's circumstances had made him realize he needed to step forward before a chef that could recognize him came through the door, like Chef Renard had done.

"You did a good job with that, *ma chère*."

"I did. I don't want to talk about the show though. Thank you for being so supportive about everything. It was nice to look over and know that you were on my side," she said.

"No problem."

She ambled over to the rail and studied the City and beyond. "It's easy to forget that we're a part of something so huge. I've seen more people here today than I normally see in my neighborhood in a year. I mean I like my quiet little life. Is New Orleans like this?"

"The French Quarter is busy all the time. It's a bit like New York, but the Garden District…that's where I live, it's quiet like the little neighborhood you described."

"Do you think you'll head back there when the competition is over?" she asked.

"I don't know," he said, but the truth was yes. He had so many new ideas for Gastrophile. But he couldn't share them with Staci. And that drove home the fact that this wasn't as real as he'd been pretending it was.

"Really?" she asked. "I'd think you'd have some idea of what your next move will be."

There was something in her tone that bothered him. It was as if she were questioning his honesty and okay, he knew he wasn't being up front with her. He knew that everything he felt and worried over stemmed entirely from the fact that if he were being honest he'd tell her all about Gastrophile and ask her to move home with him.

Frankly, he was tired of running.

"Sorry, it's just that you might sell your interest in Sweet Dreams and then we'd both be without a job. Where would that leave us?"

She stepped away from him and he knew without being told that he'd said the wrong thing. "I guess that pretty much sums it up. Why didn't you just say when the show is over, so are we?"

"Because I don't want that to be the case," he said, feeling trapped and knowing he had no one but himself to blame. If he'd been a different sort of man he wouldn't need external praise to know he was good at what he did. But he wasn't. And this show had been the only way to know if he was the same quality of chef as his father, uncles and grandfather.

He wanted to be worthy of their name, he needed to know his place in the culinary dynasty had been earned and not given, but today seeing the hurt and disappointment in Staci's eyes, he acknowledged, he'd give it all up if he could find a way to smooth over everything with her without having to reveal what he'd done.

But he was a realist and knew that would never happen. So he had to make a decision of what to tell her and he knew that the more of his soul he laid bare now the easier it might be for her to forgive him later.

"I do want you to come to New Orleans with me," he said. "But I was afraid to say that."

STACI GUESSED SHE SHOULD be careful when she pushed Remy. He always did something that was unexpected and inviting her to come to New Orleans was no exception. Even though he hadn't really invited her to come with him. He'd just said it was what he wanted.

"Why didn't you just ask me then?" She didn't see why it would be hard for him. He had nothing to lose. Or was he not sure that she'd accept him. He didn't have a kitchen to return to. "Listen, if you're worried about not having a gig, it's not a big deal. Once this show airs everyone in the country is going to be beating down your door. You'll be able to choose your assignment."

He reached over and rubbed his thumb over her lower lip before kissing her so sweetly that she felt wrapped in some emotion she was afraid to name.

"Thank you. Your offer means everything to me. But I don't think it's fair to ask you to give up your family and friends to move across the country with a man you aren't committed to."

"I understand. Just so you know if you asked me to move to New Orleans and give our relationship a real try, I'd say yes."

She felt braver than she had been in the last five years. Since she'd talked Alysse into starting Sweet Dreams with her. It had been so long since she'd risked anything, which was why she'd signed up for the show and it was Remy that was the challenge that made her feel alive. Remy and the way he inspired her to cook better. She had never felt this completely into another person before.

She was dancing around naming the emotion because once she said it, she'd be just like her mother and grand-mother. She'd have fallen in love with a man and Staci wasn't entirely sure she knew him and could trust him.

"Then I'm asking," he said. "At the end of the competition, will you move to New Orleans with me?"

She took a deep breath and held it. All the rash decisions she'd made in her life flashed before her eyes and she knew that this one was the smartest one of all.

"Yes," she said. "But I reserve the right to change my mind."

"No," he challenged her, shaking his head. "No matter what happens, you and I have made a deal to give each other a try. I asked and it was hard to do. You're either in this with me or not at all."

"I'm in it," he said.

He smiled and kissed her again. "This calls for a celebration!"

"It does?" she asked, but then realized what she'd said. "I mean, it sure does. What should we do? We're already pretty close to the top of the world."

"I know a place I think you will like," he said. "Do you trust me?"

"I wouldn't be moving to New Orleans if I didn't," she said. Hearing the words out loud warmed her. She wondered how different leaving home would be this time. When she'd moved to Paris she'd been scared but so sure of herself. This time she wasn't scared or as sure of herself. She'd wager her grandmother would say that was age giving her some wisdom.

"That's right. Okay," he said, taking her hand in his. "Follow me."

She followed him through the gift shop where he stopped at the jewelry counter and bought her a bracelet with an Empire State Building charm on it. "This is so you'll always remember this visit."

"I don't think I'll be forgetting it any time soon."

"I hope not," he said.

They took the elevator to the lobby and Staci was full of such a feeling of love. There she said it, she thought.

"Remy?" a man called to them.

Staci heard Remy curse under his breath as he turned. The man who'd spoken looked vaguely familiar to Staci. He was about as tall as Remy and had salt and pepper-colored curly hair. His eyes were dark chocolate brown and he eyed them both intently. The woman at the man's side was slightly taller than Staci and had reddish brown hair that was perfectly coifed. She wore a Lily Pulitzer sundress and looked altogether way more chic than Staci could ever hope to.

"Do you know them?" she asked under her breath.

"Yes," he said. "They're my parents."

"Mom and Dad, this is Staci. Staci, this is my mom and dad."

"Hello," Staci said holding out her hand to the couple who each shook it in turn.

"I'm Alain," his father said. "This is Betsy."

"It's so nice to meet you. Remy has told me a few things about you," Staci said.

"That's good to hear," Alain remarked. "We know nothing of you."

"I suspect that's because we're not supposed to make any calls home," Staci said.

Remy seemed as if he wanted to run away. She gave him a what's up look, which he ignored.

"Why ever not? Most boys who run away from their responsibilities aren't forbade from calling home," Betsy said. "Unless the world has changed."

"What are you talking about?" Staci asked, dropping Remy's hand. Clearly there was more going on here than she understood.

"That our son walked out of his job and has been missing for the last three months," Alain explained. "Not a single word in that time."

She faced Remy and demanded, "What are they talking about? I thought you lost your job."

"Not exactly," he said.

"Then what is the exact story?" she persisted. "Because the picture I'm getting is of a man who hasn't been honest with me."

"I'm sorry, my dear, but who did you say you were again?" Betsy asked.

"Staci Rowland, Mrs. Stephens. I'm a competitor on a cooking show that your son is also participating in."

"Mrs. Who?"

Staci swallowed hard as the truth slowly sunk in. This wasn't one lie but something much bigger. And this guy had some serious problems if he thought…what did he think?

"Isn't that your last name? Remy has presented himself as an out of work cook from New Orleans…Remy Stephens."

"He's not out of work," Alain said. "He was promoted to Chef Patron at Gastrophile and his last name is Cruzel."

"Wait. Staci I—" Remy began.

"Too late!" Staci blurted. "Stay here and explain it all to your parents. I'm going back to the hotel. I'll give you until tonight to inform the judges of your duplicity."

"Staci!"

"No. I don't want to hear any more of your carefully concocted stories. To you they might seem amusing, but to someone who had believed them, I can assure you they aren't."

13

REMY RAN AFTER STACI but she'd disappeared into the crowd and he couldn't find her. He knew as soon as she'd turned ashen that all the joy of the day had been lost. He had tried to reach for her but Staci was small and quick and determined. Determined to put as much distance between her and him as she could.

His parents were right behind them; his dad put his hand on Remy's shoulder. He didn't want to have a conversation with them right now. Everything had come undone and in the worst possible way. He needed to sort the mess out in his head so he could do what he needed to in order to win Staci back. If that were even possible.

Without Staci cooking meant nothing to him. He was looking forward to returning to New Orleans with her by his side. Not by himself. Now that he'd found love he didn't want to go back to his old life.

"We need to talk." His father's tone was solemn.

"I know we do," Remy said. "I know, it's just I have to go after her and…"

He'd seen that look in her eyes and he knew that if

he didn't get to Staci quick everything with her would be gone. And he couldn't accept that.

"I'm sorry, dear," Betsy said, "but what was that all about?"

Remy cursed under his breath and spoke to his parents. "I can talk to you both later. I'm staying at the Marquis in Times Square."

"We want some answers now," his father repeated.

"We've been worried to death about you," his mother said.

"You'll have to wait. I've made a hell of a mess, Dad, and I have to clean it up first." He went over to his mother and hugged her and gave her a kiss on the cheek. Then did the same to his dad.

"I'm sorry," he apologized.

"This girl *must* be important," his mom said.

"More important than you know and I think I just hurt her in a way I'd been hoping not to. I've got to go," he said, waving goodbye to his parents and heading out the door. He hailed a cab and as it drove through the streets, Remy carefully scanned the crowds for a glimpse of Staci, but she wasn't to be found.

As soon as he entered the Marquis, he called Jack. This disaster was entirely of his making and maybe if he did everything he could now to mitigate it he'd still be able to save his relationship with Staci. Though he knew it wouldn't be easy.

"It's Remy. There's something I need to tell you."

"Is it something that will make our ratings soar? I know you've been dating Staci—what do you say to an on-air proposal," Jack said. "I'm actually in the bar with the judges right now and some of the other production team. Come and meet us."

Remy agreed, though completely ignored Jack's suggestion about Staci. He doubted she'd say yes to anything involving him right now unless it was his head on a platter. And he couldn't blame her. Now that he knew his secret was out he regretted not telling her sooner.

When Remy entered the bar Jack waved him over and Remy ordered a Fosters from the bartender.

There was a round of greetings from everyone and Remy sat down next to Jack and turned to the producer. He took a deep breath.

"You okay?"

"Yes, I haven't been up front with who I really am."

"What? You're kidding me, right?" Jack said. "We've got three weeks of shows in the can, Remy. Please tell me you are joking."

"I'm not. My last name isn't Stephens it's Cruzel."

Everyone in the group stopped talking when he said that and stared at him.

"Are you related to Alain?" Hamilton asked.

"He's my dad."

"Why would you do this?" Lorenz asked. "A pedigree like yours should be celebrated."

"Yes, it should," Remy said. "But I've spent my entire life being told I could cook because I'm a Cruzel. And I did because that was what was expected. Even at the CIA I was treated like a star pupil and I never knew if it was because of my skills or my name."

"You decided to try an experiment to prove you had

the Cruzel talent," Pete said. "It's an interesting idea but you've lied to us all."

"I know. I'm sorry," Remy said. "At first I wasn't even sure if I'd make it to the second round so it seemed a challenge for myself more than for you. And I wanted you all to judge my dishes, not look at me and think of my father and grandfather's cooking."

"I understood that," Hamilton said. "But what does that mean for our show?"

"I'm thinking," Jack answered. "We're going to have to talk it over, Remy. I'll let you know our decision as soon as I can. Has anyone else heard about this?"

"Staci," he said.

"Ah, is she the reason you mentioned it?" Lorenz asked.

"Yes. That and the fact that the guest judges could be anyone. I know my father won't do television but my Uncle Pierre would jump at the chance to come on. I didn't want to have another shock for you guys like Staci's today."

"That's very kind of you," Fatima said.

But he could tell as they all looked at him that they were as disappointed as Staci had been. They'd become a family on the show and Remy had been lying to them all the entire time. He knew his reasons were solid but now he just felt guilty and selfish for doing it.

"What should I do now?" Remy asked. "I'd like to find Staci."

"Is she lost?" Lorenz asked. The other man leaned forward in his seat staring over at Remy.

Remy shook his head. He felt like an idiot at how he'd handled this entire situation. But he wasn't hiding anything any more. "She didn't take the news very well and we split up. Now that you guys know the truth my priority is finding her."

Hamilton watched him through narrowed eyes and then nodded. "Go. We will text you when we need you back here."

"Thank you," Remy said.

He had signed a contract with these people and though he'd read the fine print and knew there was no reason why Remy Cruzel couldn't have entered, he wondered if they'd penalize him for misrepresenting himself.

He didn't know and honestly at this moment didn't care. He'd go on to cook again when this was done but he knew deep inside his soul that there was only one woman for him and that was Staci.

He also knew that getting her back would be the hardest thing he'd ever done. It had been hard enough to woo her the first time. Although now that the truth was out he could be Remy Cruzel. He had nothing to hide and it was time that he stopped ignoring the truth of his emotions and made Staci aware of them.

Remy Stephens had had to lie low, but Remy Cruzel didn't have to and he fully intended to take advantage of that. He strode from the hotel onto the bustling sidewalk at Times Square and for the first time let himself admit that his heart ached at the thought that he might not be able to fix this and win Staci back.

Staci ran as hard and as fast as she could. When she finally stopped she realized that she'd been crying. Not silent ladylike tears, but belting sobs.

She'd had it all for a few brief seconds, she thought.

She had protected herself for so long, figured she'd been smarter this time by making Remy…what? She hadn't done anything right. She'd fallen in love with the wrong man as surely as her grandmother and her mother had done. It was sad really that another generation of Rowland woman had followed the same pattern.

She should have stayed to herself. She should have just focused on her cooking.

"You okay?" a stranger asked.

She nodded and started walking. She probably looked like something from a zombie apocalypse movie. She'd had on the camera-ready make-up, which was thick, and now it had to be ruined by her tears.

She found a Starbucks and went into the bathroom. Once she locked the door she stood in front of the mirror.

She hated the raw pain on her face, but forced herself to keep staring so that she'd always remember the real thing that Remy had given her. It was heartbreak. She needed to never forget what this felt like.

The worst part of learning that Remy had lied about everything he was from the second they met—was that she still loved him.

She buried her head in her hands and let the sobs out. She cried for all the half-formed dreams that had been floating around in the back of her mind. She cried for the little girl inside of her that had for a brief instant thought that maybe all those books she'd read as a kid had been right and that a girl like Staci could be truly happy.

She cried because she knew when she left this bathroom she'd never let herself be this weak again.

The logical part of her mind was trying to take over but the weepy woman inside her couldn't let go. Staci kept replaying the scene with Remy and his parents over and over again in her head.

She pulled out her phone and called her one true friend.

"Sweet Dreams, home of the incredible red velvet dream cupcakes. This is Alysse speaking, how may I help you?"

"It's Staci," she said. Her voice sounded deeper than normal and so rough that she was surprised by it.

"What's wrong? Where are you? Do you need me to come to Malibu?" Alysse asked.

Staci felt the love immediately from Alysse, her sister of the soul. "Everything's wrong. I'm in New York, in a bathroom…Remy has been lying to me all along."

"Is he married?"

"What? No. I mean, I don't know. I have no idea," Staci blurted. The lies that he'd told her now took on even more disturbing connotations.

"Okay, start from the beginning and tell me everything," Alysse said.

Staci took a deep breath. Just having Alysse there made things a little easier.

"Remy is part of the Cruzel family. He's been lying about who he is on the show."

"Why?"

"I don't know," Staci said.

"He could have entered the competition as Remy Cruzel, so why make up a fake name?" Alysse asked. "You have to find out."

"He lied to me," Staci said. "I can't see beyond that. I don't care what his reasons were. He told me he was a man of honor."

"He's a dirt bag," Alysse said. "I'm making you a tray of brownies and sending them to you."

"You can't. I'm not even supposed to be talking to anyone back home. I just don't know what to do. I think I love him, Aly. For the first time I thought I'd met a man who got me, you know?"

"Oh, honey, I do know. I'm so sorry."

There was only silence on the line. She couldn't help but feel like there was no hope for her and Remy. "Everyone knows we've been dating."

"I'm sure they will all be kind to you," Alysse said.

"You always were so trusting of others," Staci said. She knew that having Remy's lie exposed in front of the others was going to be hard. She didn't want their sad looks.

"I want to run away."

"If that's what you think you should do, but you're not someone who lets their problems drive them into hiding. You're a fighter, Staci Rowland," Alysse said. "Don't forget that."

She wanted to believe what her friend was telling her but a part of her, a really big part of her, was scared. She didn't know how to make this work. She didn't know how to move on from what had happened.

"What should I do?"

"I'd go back to the show and hold your head up high. You still have a competition to win, right?"

"Uh…"

"Listen," Alysse said. "I don't know how you're doing in the competition but if it were me I'd channel all that anger into kicking his butt in the kitchen. Show him and the others that you're stronger than anyone, Remy included, ever expected."

Staci liked the sound of that. She checked herself in the mirror and this time she saw the woman that Alysse had just described. Staci had been fighting her entire life and she certainly wasn't going to let Remy steal this from her. He'd shaken her faith in men. To be honest he'd probably delivered the death knell to her faith in herself.

But that was okay, she knew the way back and she'd succeed or put every last ounce of her sweat and skill into the fight.

"Thanks, Aly."

"You're welcome, honey. You know I love you. And text me later to let me know what happened."

"I will if I can. I'm going to win this thing. At least cooking is something that's just for me."

"Your cooking is for the world," Alysse said.

"You're right."

Staci hung up the phone and left the coffee shop, feeling a million times better. As she walked back to Times Square and her hotel, she felt the weight of that bracelet Remy had given her. At the concierge desk, she slipped the bracelet off her wrist and put it in a envelope to be delivered to Remy's room.

She wasn't over what had happened by any means but she was in control again and she knew that she was headed in the right direction.

TWO HOURS LATER REMY GOT the text he'd been waiting for. He hadn't been able to find Staci anywhere in the city and he suspected that when he did find her she wasn't going to be in a mood to listen.

Which put him in a really bad mood. But he tried to shake it off as he walked upstairs to the meeting room where he found Jack waiting outside.

"What's the verdict?"

"The judges want to talk to you," Jack explained. "If they agree to let you stay I'll need some extra filming time with you and I'd like to include an interview with your father."

"Why?"

"He's the reason you were pretending to be someone else, right?" Jack asked.

"Yes, but I don't think that has anything to do with the show. My parents didn't even know where I was. I needed to disappear."

"And you did, which was great for you and of course our good luck that you can cook but you still misrepresented yourself," Jack said.

"My dad won't do it, Jack. I know the man and he doesn't think much of reality TV," Remy said.

"Okay, go and see the judges. I'll try to think of an angle…but your dad disapproving of what we're doing might work."

Remy just shook his head. The room he entered was a board room with a large dark wooden table in the middle and several large armchairs set around it. On the wall were black and white photos of iconic New York City landmarks.

"Have a seat, Remy," Hamilton said from the head of the table.

Lorenz and Greg were seated on either side of him. The men were all dressed in suits and had very serious expressions. As they should, Remy thought. He pulled out a chair at the end of the table directly across from Hamilton and sat down.

"We've had a long talk and we can see why you did it," Hamilton said. "To some extent we even admire it."

"Thank you, Chef," Remy said.

"It's our decision that you can remain in the competition," Lorenz said. "We haven't spoken to the rest of the contestants yet. You will have to go on camera and explain what you were doing and why. Jack will have Fatima explain that we're giving you a second chance."

"Thank you so much," Remy said. "And again I'm sorry for what I did."

"We accept your apology. If you will move down here by us, we are going to call the rest of the contestants in for you to explain the situation to them. We have to give them a chance to adjust to this news before we all go to Ramsfeld's tonight."

"Do you think it will affect the competition and the elimination challenge?" Remy asked.

"Not on our part but we want your peers to have a chance to hear the news and discuss it. Then we can move on."

Remy nodded. He was as ready as he'd ever be to face the remaining chefs. "Is Staci with them?"

"Yes, she is," Hamilton said. "She said it didn't matter to her what name you used, she was still going to beat you."

Of course she did. Leave it to Staci to pull her defenses back around her and start showing the world her game face. He wished she would have at least let him explain privately what had been going on, instead of just assuming he was lying to hurt her.

Pete got up and left the room and Remy could only assume it was to get the other *Premier Chef* contestants. He hadn't expected to feel nervous but his palms were sweaty and he realized he'd rather have a cook off against every single one of them than have to tell them he'd lied to them.

He suspected more than one of them might want him kicked out of the competition. "Why did you decide to let me stay?" Remy asked.

"Your skills," Lorenz said. "We started this competition to find the best chefs in the country and highlight them. We've been surprised in each series how many good chefs there are around the country. To a certain extent you are the epitome of that."

"What do you mean?" Remy asked.

"The Cruzel family doesn't cook outside of New Orleans but brings Michelin judges to their part of the world. You're the head chef at a three-starred kitchen, that counts for a lot. And you didn't have to go to France or Britain or New York."

"My father thinks everyone deserves to have a fine dining establishment wherever they live," Remy said.

"I agree," Hamilton said. "That's why I do so many shows. I want audiences to know they don't have to settle for the same menu and the same dishes each time they go out for a meal. There are more choices, but unless people know about them then often the small, truly creative places close."

"I agree," Remy said.

Jack entered the room with a camera crew and placed one cameraman at either end of the room and then made sure they all had microphones on. "I might not use this but I thought it could be useful later."

The door started to open and Remy watched as his peers filed into the room. Dave and Christian on one side. Erin, Whit and Staci on the other. Staci wouldn't meet his gaze but even from this distance he could tell she'd been crying.

He felt a rush of emotions so strong that it was all he could do not to go to her. Those emotions were quelled when she finally did look at him and he saw how cold and glacier-like her gaze could be.

"There is no easy way to say it other than to tell you that Remy Stephens is not this man's real name," Greg said. "He is the son of famed Michelin starred chef Alain Cruzel. I'll let Remy explain his reasons to you and then we will listen to your comments. We have already conferred and agreed that he may remain in the competition. Remy."

Remy looked at each of the chefs remembering all the time they'd spent together in the kitchen, but it was when he looked at Staci that he felt the real need to explain. "I know we all have different reasons for entering a cooking competition, some of us are doing so to prove something to ourselves, others to prove something to the world.

"I'm in the former category in that all my life I've been treated like I was a master chef simply because of my last name. I have prepared dishes that were developed by my father and grandfather and won praise for them. But I never knew how much of the praise was because of the Cruzel name and how much of it was due to my skills.

"My father has asked me to take over as Chef Patron of Gastrophile—our family's restaurant in New Orleans. But I didn't feel ready to take on the task until I knew for certain that I was worthy of the title.

"To find out, I left New Orleans and cooked my way across the country. And when I heard about this competition and read the terms and conditions I knew I could enter and use the Anglicized version of my middle name as my last name. In truth I wasn't lying too much, I am Remy Etienne or Stephen but that's neither here nor there.

"I can only say I'm sorry that I deceived you, but I wanted a chance to be treated like everyone else and to have to prove myself one dish at a time."

14

STACI NEVER HEARD A MORE eloquent definition of a lie than the one that Remy had told. She wanted to believe that he was merely trying to recover lost ground but there was a truth to his words, she admitted. To some extent she even understood his reasoning. But her heart was a lot slower to forgive.

Remy looked as if he'd been up all night and even though it had only been a few hours since she'd seen him, he seemed tired and tense. A part of her was worried about him until she remembered that he'd lied to her. He'd known what he was doing the entire time.

She didn't have anything she wanted to say to him. She was following Alysse's advice and focusing on cooking and winning. She'd go home and lick her wounds, not to mention celebrate.

"Why are you coming clean now?" Christian asked.

Remy cleared his throat and looked directly at him. "Staci and I ran into my parents while sight-seeing and the truth came out. I also had a feeling today that Chef

Renard might have recognized me and I thought before
this went any further I should step up and clear the air."

"Did you know about this?" Whit asked under her
breath to Staci.

"Not until his parents said their last name wasn't
Stephens."

"Oh, man, I would have been pissed," Whit said.

"I was."

"Still are, if your body language is any indication,"
Whit said.

"Ladies, please ask your questions to the room," Pete
directed them.

"Sorry, Pete," Whit said. "My fault entirely. I don't
have any problems with him staying in the competition."

"Good. Does anyone have any concerns?" Pete asked.

There were a few concerns but mostly everyone
seemed to agree that by not using his legally registered
name Remy had leveled the playing field. Dave thought
that it had given Remy an unfair advantage but since
Christian and Erin both were executive chefs in well
known restaurants everyone else agreed that Remy was
fine.

"If that's everything then we have a few housekeep-
ing type items and then you can all go get dressed for
dinner at Ramsfeld's East tonight. Jack, do you want to
handle that?"

"Yes," Jack said. "Starting tonight please refer to
Remy as Chef Cruzel, rather than Chef Stephens. We
will reveal his identity as we film this week's episode
and each of you will be asked to tape a special entry

in your private video journals discussing the news and how it affected you."

"Will we have to do it now?" Staci asked. She didn't think she was ready to talk on camera about Remy's lie. Maybe once she had a few days to clear her head.

"No. When we get back to Malibu we'll do it at the house. Any other questions?" he asked.

There weren't any and they were all dismissed. Staci went immediately to the express elevator but the line was long and by the time she got on Remy was standing next to her.

"We have to talk," he said.

"I don't see why. I'm cool with everything for the show," she said as they were squeezed together along with a large group of conventioneers and a family of four. Remy was pressed right against her.

Her heart started to beat so fast and it was all she could do not to reach out and hold onto him. But then she remembered he wasn't the man she thought he was and no matter how she looked at it or how he tried to justify it, she honestly didn't know Remy Cruzel.

She pulled back and wrapped her arm around her waist. And tried to put more distance between them in spite of the crowded elevator. Remy remained still.

Here, she'd made up her mind to ignore him and now he wasn't letting her. Which just added to the anger building inside of her. When they reached their floor, she and Remy stepped off the crowded elevator.

"I'm being as civil as I can be right now, Remy," she said. She had heard his explanation and while she could buy it, she didn't want to. At least, and not right now. She felt betrayed and brokenhearted today.

"I don't want you to be civil. We need to have this out. We need to get it all sorted so we can move on. I asked you to come and live with me," he said. "That invitation still stands."

She shook her head. "And I tried to console you because you didn't have a job. Wow, that must have made you chuckle."

"I'm not that kind of man, *ma chère*—

"Don't. Do not use any endearments. We are competitors, that's all."

The elevator dinged and people got off the elevator. Remy took Staci's arm, leading her down the hall to his room. "We need to be some place private."

"Fine," she said. Agreeing that she didn't want anyone to hear the things she had to say to Remy. And now that she'd started talking to him, she had a lot to say to him.

She'd promised herself she wouldn't get upset and she was determined to keep her word.

He opened his door and gestured for her to enter. His room was set up similarly to hers with a king-size bed and two chairs over near the desk. She sat on one of them as he took the other.

"Staci, I want you to know that everything I said to you was the truth. All of it."

"Really, Remy?" she asked. Feeling that wave of emotion roiling up inside of her only this time instead of shocked tears it came out as anger.

"Do you have a job?" she asked.

"Yes, but—

"Is your last name Stephens?" she interrupted to ask him. Hurt overcoming her patience.

"No, but—"

"Would you really give it all up and move to San Diego to live with the co-owner of a cupcake bakery?" she asked. And this was the one that bothered her the most. The one she knew he'd hate to have to answer honestly.

"No, I wouldn't."

"So you kind of proved my point," she said. "You lied about the important things. The foundational things. And you said things to me that you never should have. Not until you were free to be who you really are," she said.

"If you'd give me a chance to explain then I will. I didn't lie to *you* per se I—"

"That's not helping," she said.

"Truthfully," he said. "I wasn't sure I would go back to Gastrophile. What if I'd lost all the challenges and had it proven that I wasn't the cook I thought I was. Then I wouldn't go back there and take over the restaurant. Technically, I was out of work."

"It's not the same thing and you know it."

"I do know it, which is why I'm sitting here trying to explain. I knew from the first that you were trouble."

"Don't do that," she said.

"Don't do what?"

"Make it seem like I was special. I was just gullible and bought every lie you told," she said.

THIS WASN'T GOING AT all the way that Remy had hoped it would. He saw that Staci was trying to mask her pain

over his betrayal. It should have made him be more con-
ciliatory, instead, it frustrated him.

He'd fallen in love with her. He'd invited her to come
and live with him and she acted as if it were all for nothing. That he'd done it just to make a fool of her.

"If I could go back and do things differently, I would.
But I never planned on what happened between us. And
you've got to believe me, I never lied to you about my
feelings. In fact I was more honest with you than I have
ever been with a woman. Since I couldn't share my real
last name with you I wanted to share everything else."

He didn't think she'd ever understand how badly he
now felt about the entire situation. Their flirtation had
started out so intensely. "I never meant to make love
with you that first night, but there has been this over-
whelming attraction between us, and I'm not sorry I
didn't ignore it."

"Why not?"

"Because then I would have missed out on you and
me. And I wouldn't have wanted that. Deep inside I hope
you can forgive me."

"I don't know," she said.

Staci had left behind a promising career once and re-
invented herself because of a doomed love affair. More
than likely she'd do it again.

But he could only say he was sorry so many times
and then the rest was up to her. Could she forgive and
forget? Could. Staci get beyond the things he'd said and
done to see the man he was underneath.

"I know that saying trust me isn't going to win you
back, but if we can move past this—"

"I can't. I might be able to at some point but today I just can't do it. I'm sorry, Remy. I wish we'd come into each other's lives at another time. Though to be honest I can't imagine it ever happening."

She stood and he knew she was leaving. There would be no getting her back now and no chance of working things out any further. This was it.

And so it seemed that his vacation affairs had been the smart way to go. He had thought that this romance when he was rediscovering his love of cooking and who he was, and finding this woman were meant to be.

"Before you leave, will you answer one last question for me?" he asked her.

She was standing in front of the door with her back toward him but she turned to face him. "Sure."

He looked right into her eyes and took a few steps closer.

"I know that you will never believe this, but I was taking you to my cousin's cooking school in Manhattan to show you the truth about me. I wanted you to see it and I wanted to do it in my own way."

She stepped back and reached for the door handle.

"Remy, by your very silence you took the easy way out. I'll admit I've made some bad decisions in my life but this one has cost me the most."

"I care about you, Staci," he said. "We can figure this out, make it work."

"Maybe it was because we were trapped together in the house and there was that spark between us," she said. "Because both of us should have remembered that lust isn't love. And we're both adult enough to know that affairs like this do end."

"It wasn't being trapped with you in the house. I know my feelings a lot better than that. Please believe me that I didn't set out to hurt you. The only thing I've wanted for you was a chance at happiness."

"I'll remember that," she said and then opened the door and walked away.

STACI KNOCKED EVERYONE'S socks off and won the next two weeks of challenges. She kept thinking about what Remy had said to her. It was impossible not to think about it or about him. After all she was living in the same house with him. They'd returned to Malibu but everything was different now. Especially as they entered this last week of competition and everyone had been eliminated except for her, Christian and Remy.

A part of her was glad Remy was still here because she wanted him to see that he hadn't broken her spirit. But another, secret part of her was just glad he was still around because even though it made her ache a little inside she knew she'd miss him if she couldn't see him every day.

It was Sunday and starting tomorrow they'd have an intensive cook-off where they'd be judged and earn points every day. At the end of the week the two chefs with the most points would go up against each other in a three-course meal.

Staci stiffened her spine and met the others in the living room. She took a seat at the opposite side of the room from Remy.

"Staci, that's not necessary," he said.

"Just trying to be smart," she said. "I'm hoping to win this by next week."

"I hope you do, too," he said quietly.

Christian arrived and then a moment later Jack did. "Good news, guys, tonight you will be dining at Hamilton Ramsfeld's house. He and Lorenz are fixing dinner for you. They've invited some special guests along and instead of making you wait until we get to Hamilton's place I've brought the guests here to meet you."

Jack went back outside. Staci looked at Remy and Christian and they both shrugged.

"At least they aren't taping this," Christian said, glancing around to confirm that there weren't any cameras.

"That's one small blessing," Remy agreed.

They heard the door open and then the sound of footsteps on the marble foyer. Jack's voice was a low rumble as he gave directions to whomever he had with him. The next minute a group of three people were standing before them. In the middle was Alysse.

Staci was so happy to see her best friend she almost started crying. She noticed that Remy's dad stood next to Alysse and a tall, thin woman with mocha colored skin stood on the other side.

"Everyone this is Alexi Montrell, Christian's wife. Alysse Dresden, Staci's best friend and Alain Cruzel, Remy's father," Jack announced. "You have the rest of the afternoon free. Be back here in the living room dressed casually at five."

Jack turned to leave as Christian rushed to Alexi's

side and lifted her off the ground in a big hug. Watching them made Staci wish that things had turned out differently for her and Remy.

"Hey, girl. I've missed you," Alysse said, catching her in a warm hug.

"I've missed you, too," Staci said, welcoming her friend.

"I brought brownies with me. Want to go somewhere and chat?" Alysse asked.

"May I interrupt?" Alain asked. "I'd really like the chance to speak to you, Staci."

The last thing she wanted was a heart-to-heart with Remy's dad but she had to admit she was intrigued. "All right. If Alysse doesn't mind."

"Oh, I don't," Alysse said. "I've got a few things I'd like to say to Chef Remy."

Immediately, Remy looked worried.

Staci half smiled at that and followed Remy's dad into the next room where there was a seating area.

"I'm sorry for butting in just then but we never got properly introduced," he said. "And I really wanted to talk to you again."

"I'm Staci Rowland," she said. "I hope you will forgive the way I acted in New York. You and your wife were a surprise to me. The entire thing with Remy was a mess."

"Yes, it was. Betsy and I both feel to blame for how things happened that day," he said. "Please accept our apologies for everything."

"You have nothing to apologize for," she said. "Remy is responsible for all this."

"Yes, he is. I understand that he felt pressured by me to do something he wasn't ready for."

"I don't know what Remy told you about us, but he had shared certain stories with me. I think the expectation of always living up to or rather cooking up to your reputation took its toll on him. I was just in the wrong place at the wrong time."

"I don't know about that," Alain said. "Maybe you were in the right place."

"How do you figure?"

"Remy told me that you and he were involved," Alain said.

"He did?"

"Yes and his mother and I were happily surprised that you were. We've never met anyone Remy dated," he said. "But yourself."

"You technically didn't meet me either," she said.

"We would have. Remy said he invited you to move to New Orleans."

The words still caused a pang in her heart. She had relived that moment every night in her dreams. Except the ending was always different. She knew that she was still hung up on Remy.

It was what had convinced her that her feelings for him were genuine.

"Yes, but that's not in the cards now," she said.

"It could be. I want you to come to New Orleans and work for me when the show is over. Give yourself a chance to get to know Remy again," Alain said.

She smiled at the older man because she remembered the father that Remy had described and she knew that Alain was here to do whatever he could to ensure his son's happiness. And she guessed hers as well. But Alain couldn't invite her to New Orleans. Remy had to.

And it was only then that she'd know if they had been in the right place to meet each other.

"That is a very kind offer," she said.

"But you are going to turn it down," he finished for her.

"Yes I am. I don't want to go there unless Remy and I resolve things. My home is San Diego. I don't have many blood relatives living there but I have my friends."

"I understand," Alain said. "I had to ask."

"Why?"

"Because our son has never been in love before and we wanted to meet the woman who inspired such devotion in him."

Alain made to leave. Could this be real?

"How do you know that? Did he tell you he felt that for me?"

"No. He told us by what he didn't say."

Staci wanted to believe him but she'd already been played for a fool. Except that if Remy loved her and she knew she loved him didn't they deserve the chance to be together?

15

STACI'S FRIEND AND BUSINESS partner, Alysse, was anything but sweet or dreamy when she cornered him on the balcony. Remy accepted her hard glare. He knew he deserved it.

"Okay, you had your reasons, Remy, but really, lying to Staci…it was the worst thing any man could do to her. And she thought you were different," Alysse began. "I told myself I'd be civil. Promised Jay that I wouldn't threaten you with bodily harm, but I want to. How could you?"

"I'm glad you're angry on her behalf, you should be. She's your friend. I didn't mean to hurt her," Remy said. "I wish I'd done things differently."

"You still care about her," Alysse said.

"Yes, I do. I am not going to let her keep me away. I've been giving her some space because of the competition but I intend to convince her that she belongs in my arms as soon as this is over," he said.

"Fine. I can live with that," Alysse said.

"You can?"

"Yes. I thought…well, some not nice things about you, but I am pretty good at telling when someone is being sincere and you are," she said. "Want a brownie?"

"Aren't those for Staci?" he asked.

"They were but I see now that you and I are going to have to plot and plan and come up with an excellent way for you to make it up to her."

Remy was surprised at the way she said it. "We're a team?"

"Yes, of course we are. Staci's been alone, independent for so long. We have to stick together. She's a tough nut," Staci said.

"She sure is. What'd you have in mind?" Remy asked. He liked Staci's friend and he could see why the two women would work well together. They were nothing alike, total opposites in looks and temperament but there was a good solid core in both women. A determination to get things done.

"It'll take a big gesture on your part. Staci's not going to believe it unless you do," Alysse said. "Plus, you did break her heart."

"I know that. I don't know about big gestures," he said. It wasn't his style. Still, for Staci he'd do anything it took.

He thought if he could get close enough to get her into his bed he could show her how strong his feelings were for her. They had a bond between them that even this kind of mess couldn't weaken.

"It doesn't have to be writing her name in the sky or telling her how you feel on a Jumbotron. A big gesture just has to come from the heart and it has to be at the right time."

Intimate thoughts of Staci led him to recognize that he was going to have to tell her how he felt first. Suddenly, it seemed so easy.

He'd never told Staci that he loved her. He'd done everything but that because he'd been afraid to risk getting hurt. But by being afraid and keeping her in the dark, he'd isolated her. He'd made her feel like he didn't care for her at all. He knew what gesture she needed and he had the perfect solution for when to make it.

"I've got an idea. And it will only work if we both cook our hearts out this week and make it to the finals."

"I hope you do," Alysse said.

"Staci's waiting for you inside," Alain said as he joined them on the patio.

"Thanks." Alysse stood. "Good luck, Remy. With everything."

For the first time since New York he felt a surge of hope. He now knew how to win Staci back and he would use every skill he had to ensure it happened. He'd show her in a big way.

"You look very serious, son," Alain said.

"I am, Dad. For once I think I understand why you want to retire and spend more time with Mom," Remy said.

Alain laughed. "Glad to hear it. Tell me about the cooking you've been doing. Do you have new ideas for the restaurant?"

Remy did tell his father about the new ideas he had but his mind wasn't on Gastrophile. It was on Staci and the future that he craved. He knew now that there was nothing he wouldn't do. Nothing that could stand in the way of him winning her back.

Dinner that night was uneventful. Remy watched Staci all night long. He couldn't help himself. He desperately needed her back in his arms.

"Why are you watching me like that?" she asked, when Christian and the others were preoccupied.

"Because I want you and I'm hoping to talk you into meeting me on the balcony like you did the first night we were in the house," he said.

She wet her lips with her tongue and he wanted to groan as he could think of nothing but how she tasted and just how long it had been since he kissed her.

"Sex won't make everything better," she said.

"It can't make anything worse." He frowned. "Sorry, I've missed holding you in my arms."

"I've missed that, too," she said, "But this is the last week of competition and I don't want to mess anything up. Maybe we can talk about this next week."

He smiled, knowing that by this time next week he'd have won her back if all went according to plan.

THE NEXT SEVEN DAYS WERE the most intense of Staci's life. Even though nothing had changed between her and Remy, Staci felt more positive toward the chances of them having a relationship when the competition was over. She sensed that he wanted to start again and she knew that she did. But that was going to have to wait until they were done cooking.

On Wednesday both Christian and Remy were in the

lead but on Thursday it was a dessert cook-off and she overtook them both and claimed the lead. Remy edged out Christian to claim the second spot in the final.

Friday morning dawned bright and sunny in California and as she and Remy entered the *Premier Chef* studios and went up in the elevator they both looked at each other remembering their first day here.

Remy hit the stop button on the elevator.

"What are you doing?"

"Giving us the chance to start over."

"Truly?"

"Yes."

"Okay, hi there, I'm Staci Rowland."

"Ah, the cupcake baker. Nice to meet you, cupcake girl," he said.

She shook her head and smiled at him. It had been so long since he'd called her that. She missed it, she realized.

"I'm Remy….Remy Cruzel," he said. "I'm the Executive Chef at Gastrophile in New Orleans."

"Of the famous Cruzels?" she asked.

"One and the same. I'm here to prove I can cook but now that I'm meeting you…cooking is actually the farthest thing from my mind."

"I didn't see that in your bio," she said.

"That's because I'm keeping my true identity a secret but I have a feeling I can trust you."

"Trust is a big thing for me," she said.

"I can understand that," he said. "I—"

She fake stumbled into him and he caught her. She gave him a quick kiss on the cheek but he turned his head and kissed her full on the lips instead. He held her tenderly in his arms. She had missed the feel of his arms around her, too. He drew her closer to him.

"That's what I wanted to do when you fell into me that first time," he said.

"I would have called the cops," she said.

"Would you have?" he asked. "My kisses are pretty good. Maybe you've forgotten."

He leaned down and kissed her again slowly and passionately and she wrapped her arms around him, wanting to hold him close. But the elevator doors opened and they sprung apart.

"Ladies first," Remy said.

Heading down the hallway to the studio, they entered and found that the entire cast had been invited back. Staci had a quick catch-up with Vivian and then it was time to get ready for the taping.

They were both miked and had stage make-up put on and then sent to their stations. Staci had been practicing her menu in her mind since the beginning of the week. The dishes they'd prepared throughout the week would be the ones they'd make today. She knew she had to improve on her appetizer course, which she'd lost to both men.

"Welcome, Chefs. It seems like a long time ago when you first stood in this room and now we're down to two would be Premier Chefs left standing before us. Chef Rowland and Chef Cruzel," Hamilton said.

"You two have impressed us by winning Quick Cooks and challenges but mostly you've won us over with your fabulous dishes," Lorenz said.

"Today is your last chance to out-do the competition and claim the title of Premier Chef," Pete said.

"Chefs, it is time to start cooking," Fatima chimed in. "The cameras are rolling. We'll begin with appetizers and you will each have thirty minutes to prepare them. Your time starts now."

Staci cooked her heart out but Remy's dish won five points and hers only four. The next round was a tie with them both scoring five points each. Staci was nervous and so afraid she might lose but then she thought, as she watched Remy cooking, that she'd gained more the last six weeks than she'd ever expected to.

At the dessert round, she was completely focused and felt confident. Remy went first, presenting his dessert to the judges and after a few minutes they asked for hers. The judges tasted her Crème Freche Torte and sent her and Remy to the main studio to await the final results. There, Remy quickly pulled her into his arms away from the cameras and the audience.

"Now it's time for me to do what I should have done in New York when we were at the Empire State Building. In my heart I knew then that I loved you more than life itself. I wanted to tell you but was scared that if I did and you later found out about my lie you would never believe in our love.

"And while it's too late to change the past," he said, staring into her eyes. "The future is ours and I mean to spend the rest of my life with you. Will you give me another chance at being the man of your dreams?"

"Yes, Remy," she said. "I will. I love you, too and

can't think of anything I'd like better than being with you."

When it was time, Remy and Staci re-entered the studio holding hands.

"So perhaps we have something else to celebrate?" Hamilton asked.

"Yes," they said in unison.

"Good, now maybe we can get on with our show," Hamilton said smiling at both of them.

Fatima announced, "The dessert round has been the toughest yet and the hardest to judge but after much deliberation we are happy to announce that Staci Rowland is our winner!"

Staci turned to Remy who hugged her and kissed her and lifted her off the ground. "I knew you could do it."

"Not without you," she said with a smile, knowing she had truly found it all. Now that she had the Premier Chef title and had put the past behind her, her future was filled with love, and the man of her very own sweet dreams.

* * * * *

Have Your Say

You've just finished your book.
So what did you think?

We'd love to hear your thoughts on our
'Have your say' online panel
www.millsandboon.co.uk/haveyoursay

- 🌹 Easy to use
- 🌹 Short questionnaire
- 🌹 Chance to win Mills & Boon®
  goodies